The RIDE of our Lives

The Ride of our *Lives*

And Other Short Stories

CAROLYN CROOP

Copyright © Carolyn Croop.

All rights reserved. No part of this book may be reproduced in any form or by any electronic or mechanical means, including information storage and retrieval systems, without permission in writing from the publisher, except by reviewers, who may quote brief passages in a review.

ISBN: 978-1-64999-001-3   (Paperback Edition)
ISBN: 978-1-64999-002-0   (Hardcover Edition)
ISBN: 978-1-64999-000-6   (E-book Edition)

Some characters and events in this book are fictitious. Any similarity to real persons, living or dead, is coincidental and not intended by the author.

Book Ordering Information

Phone Number: 347-901-4929 or 347-901-4920
Email: info@globalsummithouse.com
Global Summit House
www.globalsummithouse.com

Printed in the United States of America

DEDICATION

To Everyone and Anyone
Who Believes in the Power of Their Dreams

Contents

Dedication v
Forward xiii

The Ride of Our Lives 1
    Chapter 1 3
    Chapter 2 5
    Chapter 3 7
    Chapter 4 8
    Chapter 5 9
    Chapter 6 10
    Chapter 7 12
    Chapter 8 13
    Chapter 9 14
    Chapter 10 15
    Chapter 11 16
    Chapter 12 17
    Chapter 13 18
    Chapter 14 19
    Chapter 15 20

The Two of Me 21
    Chapter 1 23
    Chapter 2 24
    Chapter 3 25
    Chapter 4 26
    Chapter 5 27
    Chapter 6 28
    Chapter 7 29
    Chapter 8 30

Hands of Time	31
[Book I]	33
Chapter 1	35
Chapter 2	36
Chapter 3	38
Chapter 4	39
Chapter 5	40
Chapter 6	42
Chapter 7	43
Chapter 8	44
[Book II]	45
Chapter 1	47
Chapter 2	48
Chapter 3	49
Chapter 4	50
[Book III]	51
Chapter 1	53
Chapter 2	54
Chapter 3	55
Get a Life	57
Chapter 1	59
Chapter 2	60
Chapter 3	61
Chapter 4	62
Chapter 5	63
Chapter 6	64
Chapter 7	65
Mother Nature's Revenge	67
Chapter 1	69
Chapter 2	70
Chapter 3	72
Chapter 4	74
Chapter 5	75

A Mysterious Salesman 77
    Chapter 1 79
    Chapter 2 81
    Chapter 3 83
    Chapter 4 85
    Chapter 5 87
    Chapter 6 90
    Chapter 7 92

The Disappearance of Eve 93
    Chapter 1 95
    Chapter 2 96
    Chapter 3 98
    Chapter 4 100
    Chapter 5 101
    Chapter 6 103
    Chapter 7 104
    Chapter 8 106
    Chapter 9 108
    Chapter 10 109
    Chapter 11 111
    Chapter 12 113
    Chapter 13 114
    Chapter 14 115

Alien Science Project 117
    Chapter 1 119
    Chapter 2 120
    Chapter 3 121
    Chapter 4 123
    Chapter 5 124
    Chapter 6 125
    Chapter 7 126
    Chapter 8 127
    Chapter 9 128
    Chapter 10 130
    Chapter 11 132

I Traveled Far Within A Book 133
    Chapter 1 135
    Chapter 2 136
    Chapter 3 138
    Chapter 4 139

Broken Dreams and Magic Schemes 141
    Chapter 1 143
    Chapter 2 144
    Chapter 3 145
    Chapter 4 146
    Chapter 5 148
    Chapter 6 149
    Chapter 7 150
    Chapter 8 151
    Chapter 9 152

Heart for Hire 153
    Chapter 1 155
    Chapter 2 156
    Chapter 3 157
    Chapter 4 158
    Chapter 5 159
    Chapter 6 160
    Chapter 7 161
    Chapter 8 162
    Chapter 9 163
    Chapter 10 164
    Chapter 11 165

A Holiday Trilogy 167
    Chapter 1 169
    Chapter 2 170
    Chapter 3 171
    Chapter 4 172

A Thanksgiving Story: The Prayer 173
    Chapter 1 175
    Chapter 2 177
    Chapter 3 178

A Christmas Story: Baby, Please Come Home 179
    Chapter 1 181
    Chapter 2 182

Class Act 183
    Chapter 1 185
    Chapter 2 186
    Chapter 3 187
    Chapter 4 188
    Chapter 5 189
    Chapter 6 190
    Chapter 7 191
    Chapter 8 192
    Chapter 9 193
    Chapter 10 194
    Chapter 11 195
    Chapter 12 196
    Chapter 13 197
    Chapter 14 198
    Chapter 15 199
    Chapter 16 200
    Chapter 17 201

Forward

I will be the first to admit that not all of my writing meets my own personal criterion. Like all artists and creators, some works are masterpieces while others turn out less than the desired standards. It takes a lot of guts, hard work, and risk taking to publish a completed project or work of art. With that being said, some of my work was written during the elementary stages of my writing. Some do not meet my current standards.

Whether good or bad, I chose to publish nearly all of my writing to display the progression of my work. I partially did this in an attempt to show others that first endeavors don't always succeed. If you set your mind to it, you can improve little by little each step of the way.

I am proud of my writing achievements and the outcome of this book. Several stories derived from rhyming stories that I wrote early on. One even originated as a music playlist. Hence, not all of the stories within this book were first attempts.

I would be happy if even one person viewed me as a leader and role model to the path of achieving their dreams. Keep in mind that it is okay to fail. Keep the faith and keep trying. Always keep your dreams alive!

THE RIDE OF OUR LIVES

A Story of Friendship

Chapter 1

This is how the story ends. I had three lifelong true best friends. We were known as the "four-ever friends". We stayed friends until the bitter end.

The story of our friendship begins here. On a summer day before attending the county fair, my friends and I fixed our hair. The "four-ever friends" were eight years old. Even so, we still cared about our appearance in front of boys.

As we walked about the fair, the four of us noticed that no one was riding the roller coaster.

The man in charge yelled in our direction saying, "Free ride."

I later referred to the man as a con artist. The reason for his nickname was that I learned in life, there are no free rides. Everything bears a cost, including friendship.

Grace, Nicole and Abigail were my friends' names. I am Jane, a ninety-two year old grandmother living in a nursing home. I'm telling this story for the sake of my granddaughter, Victoria. She prefers to be called Tori. You see, the "four-ever friends" hopped on the free roller coaster ride that day at the fair. We had the ride of our lives for the rest of our lives. Now Tori wants to venture on a crusade with her friends. She has always admired me as her role model, so I must tell her the value and the pitfalls of such a ride.

Abigail was a bit of a drama queen, so it did not surprise me when she took the front seat on the roller coaster. She was typically the leader of our pack. Nicole was rather shy back then and chose to sit in back. Grace and I rode in the center together.

The ride slowly ascended up the tracks as Abigail waved and said, "Look at me!"

I heard the clanking of the roller coaster hitting the tracks, knowing full well that we would soon be at the top. From there, the ride had only one way to go and that was full speed downhill. In what seemed like a split second, we were screaming at the top of our lungs as we descended down the tracks. Suddenly, the four of us were inside a tunnel with walls of mirrors. It was shocking to see that we were all now eighteen years old! The ride led us outside the tunnel and over a few more hills before the roller coaster stopped to let us off. We thanked the con man for the ride and returned to our homes for the night.

Nicole married at age eighteen. Her husband, Andrew turned out to be a millionaire. I graduated high school with straight A's. I wasn't sure where that was going to lead me. Abigail was planning to attend college to become a journalist. I always hoped that her drinking habit wouldn't get in the way. Grace was the prettiest of the four of us. Boys were always looking in her direction and asking her out. We all lived close to one another and kept in contact. We got together about once a week for parties, shopping, or just to chat.

The four of us never attended the county fair again until we were twenty five. Sure enough, the con man was still there directing us towards the ride. We couldn't understand why no one else was on the roller coaster. We gladly took him up on his offer and rode the roller coaster again! This time, when we entered the tunnel, the mirror images showed us to be thirty-three years old. Once again, at the end of the ride, we thanked the con man. Only this time, Grace, Nicole, Abigail and I lost touch with one another afterward. We lived our lives not knowing anything about the lives of our friends.

Chapter 2

Abigail's Story

The "four-ever friends" all had our ups and downs in life. It was as though we continually rode the roller coaster. Abigail made it to the top but warned us that the ride of life may drop. She was a prime example of this topsy-turvy ride through life. I will explain.

Abigail's family appeared to be perfect to others. Her friends (Nicole, Grace and I) were the only ones who knew otherwise. Abigail's parents were wealthy and, unfortunately, they spent far too much time preoccupied with work. Abigail and her sister were ignored even at pivotal moments of their lives. It was no wonder why she turned to drinking. Nicole, Grace and I knew matters were regressing when Abigail nearly got involved in crime and drugs.

While in high school, Abigail befriended two boys who were not a good influence on her. They skipped school and drank alcohol together at times. Luckily, she confided in us that the boys were planning a robbery involving her. She was to drive the getaway car. She also told us that the boys had planned to do heroin that same evening along with Abigail. We were so glad she told us their scheme ahead of time. We gave her hugs and all of us talked her out of it.

Additionally, Abigail was on the verge of dropping out of high school. Her life seemed to have no clear direction or guidance. Nicole had always dreamed of becoming a teacher. She made the biggest impact on Abigail's decision to remain in school. After all, Abigail was a remarkably bright girl. As stated before, she had a desire to obtain a degree in journalism. We all wanted to see her succeed. She did just that.

Abigail attended a local university and earned her Bachelor's Degree. We were so proud of her, yet angry at the same time. It seems her classmates had a bet going on behind her back. They were confident that Abigail would never make it to graduation due to her drinking habit.

They placed bets that she would wind up becoming a homeless drunk. I was furious to find this out. On the contrary, Abigail was unassailable and never showed anger. Her inside strength is what I admired the most about Abigail.

Soon after she graduated college, Abigail became a star reporter for a local news station. I wondered how many lost the bet. By age thirty three, she was clearly riding at the top of life's roller coaster. She had a very promising future ahead of her.

Chapter 3

Nicole's Story

Raised in a large, close-knit family, Nicole was the youngest and earned the nickname of "daddy's little girl." Although her father spoiled all of his children, Nicole felt a special bond with him. Whenever she experienced any type of problem, he made it his priority to help her resolve it.

Nicole was often seen smiling and helping out others. She married Andrew at age eighteen, right after high school. By age nineteen, they had a son, Nicholas. She used to call me to ask for parenting advice. Nicholas was a handful. He was a hyperactive child. I was never quite sure what to tell her. I think she just needed someone to listen. She was doing everything she was supposed to be doing. She drove Nicholas to friends' houses, to the doctor, and paid close attention to him.

Nicole, Andrew and Nicholas attended church every Sunday. They became close friends with the minister who led them on the right path in life. Andrew earned his college degree in finance and, soon after, became a Wall Street tycoon. Andrew knew where to invest their money as they were able to purchase a mansion. By age thirty, Nicole was also able to go to college and earn her degree. Her childhood dream of becoming a teacher came full circle when she was hired to teach children who were hard of hearing.

Nicole was the only one of the four of us who didn't have a battered soul. Her life really was perfect. The best part of Nicole was that she didn't flaunt her wealth or come across as better than anyone. Like I said, she was always helping others.

Chapter 4

Grace's Story

After high school, Grace was hired at a fashion design company, earning great pay. She married her high school sweetheart, Dave at age twenty four. I was never too fond of Dave. I felt that he mistreated her by belittling her and degrading her with name calling. I could not understand what she ever saw in him. Dave liked spending money and both were not good at money management. Her world seemed dark and gray and went from bad to worse. You see, their son died at one month old, when Grace was only twenty seven. She stopped believing in God.

Grace hurt deep inside but never let it show. She even knew that Dave was cheating on her and just let it slide. In some ways, the couple matured after experiencing the death of their son. By age thirty, Dave had curbed his spending habits and they both acquired better money management skills. Grace and Dave each had lucrative jobs and were able to purchase a house by the ocean. It was in their new town that Grace visited a church and relearned of God and the power of prayer.

After two years, Grace was ready to have another child. Previously, she thought she was done having children forever. She felt that she could not take the risk of losing another child. The pain was nearly unbearable. Dave and Grace talked it over and both agreed to try again.

Chapter 5

Jane's Story

There was a secret I kept from my friends. Raised by both of my parents, I was routinely beaten by my father. This caused me to develop deep depression. I habitually hid the bruises by wearing long-sleeved shirts and pants to cover them up. I never let Abigail, Nicole or Grace know the truth. The beatings ceased when I began dating my first boyfriend which was also around the same time my parents divorced.

My boyfriend and I met in high school at age seventeen and married at age twenty two. Like Grace, we too purchased a house by the ocean. There was, however, no way to stop the heartache of my divorce which occurred after my mental breakdown. This happened at age thirty after having two children.

During my stay in the hospital, I was first diagnosed with postpartum depression. Later, the doctors re-diagnosed me as having bipolar disorder and severe depression. My mind was on a rampage. My thoughts were constantly racing and continually changing. I was confused by everything anyone said to me. The doctors tried different medications for months, none of which seemed to work. I later learned that I carry the bipolar gene and that severe stress had triggered it. I would assume my hostile childhood played its part.

I had shown some improvement a year later; however, I was still not fully recovered. Experiencing unclear thinking, I married again at the first chance I had. I realized far too late that the man I married was only using me for my money and house by the ocean. He was considerably like Dave, Grace's husband. Both were narcissists. I was abused once again in life and shortly after the marriage, I lost all my savings and home. When I also lost my job, the end of my second marriage followed closely behind. I was left to live in homeless shelters by myself. Once in a while, I saw my two children. They were the light of my days. I never once gave up my dream of producing a number one best selling book.

Chapter 6

What a surprise I received in the mail at age forty nine! The invitation stated to meet at the county fair.

It said, "The four-ever friends, be there!"

Abigail, Nicole, Grace and I were about to turn fifty. We would soon be celebrating our birthdays by riding the roller coaster once again. We had lost touch with one another since age thirty three. I couldn't wait to see them again and discover what their lives had been like. I then froze in place. *"What would they think of my life?, I wondered. I didn't have anything great to tell them. I had been in and out of mental hospitals since then. What could I share that was amazing? I hadn't even published one book yet."*

I spent a week contemplating my decision to go or not. I then sent back a response and bought four bracelets for me and each friend. I couldn't pass up the opportunity to regain my friendships. I had the bracelets engraved with "four-ever friends".

We had all turned fifty and the day arrived. The "four-ever friends" met at the county fair. We gave each other hugs and walked about the fair while eating cotton candy. To our surprise, the con man was still in charge of the roller coaster, waving us in his direction. He hadn't changed a bit. I don't know how it was possible, but he still appeared to be forty years old.

Once again, Abigail, Nicole, Grace and I were the only people to board the roller coaster. Like before, the ride was free; however, there was one small change. After reaching the top and zooming downward, coasting over the hills, we entered the tunnel which had no mirror. By the time the ride ended, we looked at one another and sure enough, we were still age fifty. I suppose the reason our age didn't change through the tunnel was because, by that point in our lives, we had slowed down our pace. There was no mirror since we had learned not to hurry through life

The four of us had a blast riding the roller coaster. Although afterward, we decided to take a break and sit at a picnic table while catching up with one another. We wanted to know what had happened to each friend's life while we were apart. After hearing each one's story, we vowed to one another never to part again. I found out that in our forties, everyone of us had a mid-life crisis. We knew it would have been easier to bear if we had been there to support one another. Abigail was the first to tell us about her life from ages thirty three to fifty.

CHAPTER 7

Abigail's Life (Ages 33-50)

Abigail had lost her job as a news reporter as I had feared. She was fired due to her excessive drinking problem. However, she eventually reached the top in life once again, shortly after meeting Bob. He became the love of her life and helped her to recover.

Abigail confided in us at the fair that she could never have children. We never knew this about her. After overcoming her alcohol addiction, she married Bob and they adopted a boy named Pierre. He was fourteen at the time of his adoption and blessed to have such wonderful new parents.

Pierre had lived in several different foster homes and shelters, in addition to once being homeless. Abigail and Bob saw great potential in him. They took a chance on Pierre and gave him a life like none he ever knew before. Abigail's son filled a void and gave her a sense of reward by helping someone else. A strong family bond developed. Abigail ultimately felt contentment within all aspects of her life.

Chapter 8

Nicole's Life (Ages 33-50)

Nicole's life was always perfect, so it was shocking to discover she was unhappy in her early forties. Her father died when she was forty one. He had left behind a four-leaf clover charm along with a note. Each leaf represented each of the "four-ever friends". Her father knew how much our friendships meant to Nicole. He had hopes that someday we would rekindle our close friendship bond.

During Nicole's mid-life crisis, she walked away from the church. This surprised me as Nicole had always been a faithful church goer. Nicole's depression grew deeper so her husband, Andrew arranged for her to begin therapy sessions. She was later diagnosed with clinical depression and placed on medication. Andrew stayed by her side throughout it all. Eventually, he even got Nicole to return to church. It was a long, hard journey, but Nicole made it through with flying colors. She showed no signs of depression during our time at the fair. Abigail, Grace and I told her to reach out to us next time she feels down. We were not about to ever break apart again.

Chapter 9

Grace's Life (Ages 33-50)

At age thirty-six, Grace was blessed with another child, Colleen. She had made the right decision to have a child after the death of her first baby. Colleen brought much joy into Grace's life. Unfortunately, her husband Dave had not changed a bit. His narcissistic behavior began taking a toll on Grace. She always felt that she could handle the verbal abuse, although it got worse than that at times.

Grace spent her time taking care of Colleen and cleaning like a mad woman. Her home was immaculate, yet still Dave belittled her and told her it was the dirtiest house he had ever lived in. Because Colleen was now part of their family, Grace felt she could no longer live with this type of constant abuse. Grace divorced Dave and did something she had only dreamed of. She learned how to play the guitar, wrote songs, and joined a band. The first song she recorded actually made it to radio as a number one hit. Part of it went like this:

"The Sun's Ray"

Darkened skies day and night
The sun never shined after he died
It is said time heals and shines the light
Time passed
I Tried.
They lied
I cried
I see my son in the sky
The sun's ray within my eyes

Chapter 10

Jane's Life (Ages 33-50)

There isn't much to tell about my life during the years Abigail, Nicole, Grace and I were apart. I continued to live my life with mental issues, in and out of the hospital. Like my friends, I too had a mid-life crisis. The only difference was that I enjoyed it. Since I was aging gracefully, I still appeared to be a teenager to some. This was especially so after I dyed my hair with one pink streak. I occasionally went on shopping sprees with my teenage daughters as well. I think they enjoyed my mid-life crisis as much as I did since they benefited from the spending.

I dated a few men for a short period of time. One of them truly captured my heart. I don't even know what happened. We didn't have an argument or break up. We simply went our own ways and eventually stopped contacting one another.

After that short relationship, I decided to stop dating and begin writing. I wrote poetry, stories and even a novel. During that time frame, a new medication for my condition was on the market. My doctors switched me to the new drug. Within a month, I noticed a big change in my thinking. As a result, my family told me that my behavior had greatly matured. I was finally back to thinking and behaving as I had been before my breakdown.

Chapter 11

The "four-ever friends," Abigail, Nicole, Grace and I kept in contact at least once a week after attending the county fair at age fifty. I called each of them the day I received a mystery letter that was inside the mailbox in the hallway of my apartment building. The letter had a key attached and stated that my life would get better. There were instructions for me to walk outside to the parking lot at my apartment complex.

I was thrilled to find a brand new car wrapped with a bow and a note that said, "Jane, will you marry me?"

Neither the letter or the note was signed. It was wonderfully exciting yet mysterious. I had no clue who had done this.

Abigail, Nicole and Grace all acted surprised when I called to let them know about the mystery. I knew them well enough to believe that they had knowledge about who had sent the letter and car. *I thought, "They must be in on it."* Grace told me to meet her at a local bar where her band was playing. I met up with her that evening and, to my surprise, Abigail and Nicole showed up too.

We all went to the dance floor when suddenly my heart dropped. The music stopped too. There he was!

The love of my life, wearing a tuxedo said to me, "Please be my wife."

I could not stop staring into his eyes. He was the only man who made me feel shy. I then realized the room was silent waiting for my response.

I answered, "Yes."

Adam, the love of my life, and I embraced. He had been the man who had captured my heart years before. We hadn't seen each other again until that night.

The band resumed playing and days later, I started planning a wedding. Times were bright for me, as I also published books. Some reached number one and some were made into movies. Times Square even displayed a lit up billboard featuring my movies and my name. Life could not be better.

Chapter 12

Only five months after reuniting with Adam, we were married. My daughters both shared the role of Maid of Honor. I had three other bridesmaids at my wedding who were naturally Abigail, Nicole and Grace. I was married as the sun was setting by the ocean. Nothing could have been more poetically breathtaking.

Grace's band was there playing love songs. She was, at that time, the only one of the four of us who was unmarried. Her situation of being single only lasted two more years because it was at my wedding that she met Don. The two of them hit it off and eventually married too.

Chapter 13

My heart broke into pieces the day I received a fateful call. Without warning, Nicole had died at age seventy eight. The con man showed up at her funeral, and to my amazement, he even stood up at the podium to speak. After all those years, I finally discovered his name was Ernie. It was mystifying that he still appeared to be forty years old.

Ernie spoke about the "four-ever friends" and our ride on the roller coaster at the fair. He said we were the first bunch of friends to board the roller coaster. The reason no one else got on was that friendship was not free. It bears the cost of losing friends that you have chosen. I had never previously given any thought to that.

Grace died years later at age eighty three and Abigail died at age eighty nine. They had both become ill before their deaths. Although I suffer great pain from their loss, the friendship I shared with all three is something I never regret. Their memories are a monumental part of me. When my time comes, I will rest in peace knowing I lived a full life of eternal love and friendship.

Chapter 14

Adam knew how much I was hurting after the death of all three of my friends. He wanted to cheer me up one rainy day while I was at the nursing home. Adam has lived apart from me ever since I moved in here. I have health issues that he was unable to take care of himself. Thus, as hard as it is, I live here and he lives in the home we shared together.

Adam called me and told me to come outside. He said he hopes I like the rain. When I opened the door, I saw Adam sitting in a horse-drawn carriage.

He said, "How about a slow and steady ride this time my friend for life?"

I hopped onto the carriage and Adam and I held hands as we rode along. We stopped to have ice cream cones together and smiled at one another. You see, Adam knew just how I felt losing Abigail, Nicole and Grace. He had been one of a group of eight friends that was called "the great eight". He has lost most of his friends too.

I missed the bingo game at the nursing home today. I'm told I ramble on too much at times. When you're ninety-two, that's what you do. There is just one word of advice I have before I'm finished. Be true to yourself.

CHAPTER 15

My granddaughter, Tori, is ready for her crusade. She leaves today. She called to say goodbye and thanked me for telling my story. She's such a kind and thoughtful young lady. Tori and her group of friends are considered to be sweet angels. They're known as "the seven from heaven."

My grandson, Nate, is here visiting me. I've been telling him a new story. Adam just walked into my room. He's waving his hands for me to stop talking.

He brought me a bouquet of red roses and said, "I love you".

I said, "What?"

He repeated, "I love you."

I smiled and said, "I know. I just wanted to hear it one more time."

The ride of our lives charged a cost, but I was grateful to pay.

THE END

THE TWO OF ME

A Lesson on Gratitude

Chapter 1

Choices that we make determine our fate. I wondered about the path I traveled. *I asked myself, "Would I become wise too late? Were the choices I made in life the best ones?"* These thoughts consumed my head. I wanted answers and there was only one Man I could rely on to give them to me. Therefore, I asked God to show me how my fate would have played out if even one of my life choices had been made differently. Don't get me wrong. I was not completely unhappy with where I was in life. Though, could it have been better?

Just then, I heard the voices of angels intently speaking, "We will show you how your life would have been like if you had made one different choice. At a party years ago, you were given a handful of street drugs. At that instant, you had a crucial decision to make. There were simply two options which were to consume the drugs or not."

Magic dust sprinkled across my face from out of nowhere.

The angels' voices continued on by saying, "There are now two of you. We are giving you the unique opportunity to see the fate of both."

I then became myself and "Diane". Everything about the two of me was alike down to every last detail. Both Diane and I were the same inside and out.

Chapter 2

The angels sent the two of me to a pivotal moment in my past. Diane and I were at the same party. We were both handed about ten different street drugs. I chose not to consume them. Diane, on the other hand, chose differently. She thought that by taking the drugs, she would fit in with the others and that drugs might make her happy.

After ingesting the drugs, Diane began making no sense when she talked.

"I'm flying with wings," she exclaimed.

Diane was experiencing the effects from her decision to take the drugs. Meanwhile, I left the scene. I was against drugs and the people at the party were not for me. They treated me as an outcast, calling me names such as "nerd" and "loser." I ignored them and went home. Diane was left behind. The angels' voices told me of her dreadful fate.

Chapter 3

The Life of Diane

Shortly after Diane consumed the drugs, she got sick and passed out on the floor at the party. Unfortunately, it only took one time to be forever addicted to drugs. By morning, she awoke still feeling sick and groggy. The drugs had begun to wear off. No one showed compassion.

Diane left the scene by herself and wandered the streets in search of her home. When she eventually arrived, her parents lectured her for being out all night. She was sent to her room where she cried herself to sleep.

The following day, her parents gave her permission to visit her boyfriend, Brandon. Diane had hopes to one day marry him. To her surprise, Brandon turned her away. He had heard rumors about Diane's behavior at the party. Brandon had his future all planned out. Drugs were not part of it.

After breaking up with Brandon, Diane felt depressed. She wanted instant happiness and began to wonder how much drugs cost. Douglas, the boy from the party who handed her drugs, became Diane's new drug dealer.

Chapter 4

The Life of Me

After leaving the party and arriving home, I went to my room and cried. I wondered if I had made the right choice. The people at the party had appeared to be having fun. I felt alone and excluded by not participating with drugs.

The next day, I visited my boyfriend, Brandon. I told him about the party while we ate ice cream together. He hugged me and told me he was proud that I made the right choice. Two years had passed since then. I became Brandon's wife.

Chapter 5

The Life of Diane

Two years had passed. Diane found it difficult to keep a job. She had been a straight A student beforehand. It was a shame that her potential led her to jobs cleaning and mopping floors. Although, she desired to work and earn money to support her drug addiction. Her entire life revolved around drugs.

Diane and Douglas became a couple. Douglas was a drug addict too. Nearly all of their money was spent on drugs, leaving them homeless. Even in cold winter months, they lived outdoors in tents.

One fateful day, Diane overdosed. She was rushed to the hospital where she later died.

Chapter 6

The Life of Me

Because of my straight A grades, I had been hired at a lucrative company. As time continued on, I received a job promotion. I was told that I was an ideal employee and even a role model to some.

Eventually, I had two children. Brandon treated me with respect and held me high upon a pedestal. My life was perfect, although I took it for granted. I always saw the negative aspects of my life.

Everyday I drove to and from work. I became bored. *I thought, "There must be more to life."* Brandon, the children, and I went on occasional day trips. We never invested in long vacations. I pouted about the life I thought I was missing out on. I held onto jealousy of the thought that other people's lives appeared better than mine.

My negative mind frame led me to depression. I was the unhappy girl who had everything. I rarely smiled and talked without listening. Yet, Brandon still loved me.

Chapter 7

It was the month of December and a Christmastime to remember. Diane was gone and I was living the ideal life. Alone at home, I talked to the voice of an angel. She gently spoke with sorrow as she greeted me. I was shocked when the angel raised her voice to lecture me.

"Your life is full of spice. Count your blessings," she loudly said.

The angel was mean. I thought angels were always nice.

She went on to say, "Stop the pity party. You're at the height of your life. Embrace what you have."

The angel taught me not to focus on what I lacked, but to instead, be grateful. The angel said it was time for her to leave. Her name was Diane.

Chapter 8

My wish had been granted. I was given the chance to know the fate of two different versions of me. I had taken my life for granted. I learned to count my blessings each and every day. It was not too late to learn my lesson.

Nothing was missing in my life. My choices really do chart the path towards my destiny. I was grateful for the gift I received. Christmas fun with family and friends had begun.

THE END

HANDS OF TIME

A Romantic Time Travel Story

[BOOK I]

Chapter 1

Four teenagers, Tom, Ingrid, Melissa and Ed, created quite a story to be spread around the world. The four had been friends since age six. They were always seen together. One day though, they discovered an unusual clock to be forever treasured.

On a Friday evening in springtime, the friends rode in Tom's car on their way to the prom. Even though Tom, Ingrid, Melissa and Ed were only friends, they paired together as dates. They were merely five miles away from the dance hall when suddenly Tom's car broke down. He immediately called a towing company and the car was taken away.

The friends were stranded close by to a neighborhood. An old woman appeared to be spying on the teens. She was peering from her window at their situation and wanted to help. The old woman, wearing a long gown, stepped outside of her house. She invited the teens inside while they waited for a ride to the prom.

The old woman lived alone. It took hours for their ride to arrive. In the meantime, the four friends sat down in the old woman's living room. They chatted with her; although, the teens did most of the listening. The old woman seemed as though she hadn't talked to anyone in years and shared many stories. The group did not plan for what happened next.

Ed stood up from the couch and curiously looked at the surroundings. Discovering an antique clock on the wall, he lightly touched it. Suddenly, the old woman's face changed to fright as the clock began to fall. The old woman was the only person who understood exactly what had just occurred. The clock was, indeed, old fashioned; yet, it would become the center of the four friends' fate.

Chapter 2

In the niche of time, Melissa grabbed the falling clock. Immediately, the clock chimed. The four friends would soon become shocked, however. Ed was further curious and moved the clock's hands. The old woman became furious as she commanded Ed to change the clock back to its original setting.

"Turn back the clock immediately! I am insistent that the four of you take a vow to never touch the clock," said the old woman.

Just before Ed had a chance to turn the clock back, Tom received a phone call. The person on the other end was supposed to be giving the teens a ride to the prom. Instead, the person asked Tom why they were not at the dance hall yet.

Tom had a look of confusion and replied, "I called you more than an hour ago for a ride."

The person on the other end disagreed and was insistent that he never received a call asking for a ride. Tom grew frustrated and ended the call. The woman then changed the clock's hands back to their original settings. She and three of the friends stepped into the dining room where the old woman had food for them. Ed remained behind to further loom. He was highly suspicious as he inspected the premises by himself.

Ed had disregarded the old woman's wishes. He moved the clock's hands back and forth. When he did this, he discovered that time itself moved back and forth. Ed was confident that he had stumbled upon a grand discovery.

When Ed's friends and the old woman returned, Ed shared his news that the clock was capable of changing time to future and past.

"Do not misuse the clock by changing the hands," said the old woman.

"Were you already aware of the clock's abilities?," asked Ingrid as she addressed the old woman.

"It must be kept a secret that the clock can move time to future and past. Do not live to regret your decisions and believe that changing time is a blast," said the old woman.

The four friends did not ask anymore questions; although, they were not about to obey the old woman's commands. They were eager to test the clock for themselves. Soon the friends would be venturing to the future and past.

Chapter 3

Tom, Ingrid, Melissa and Ed whispered amongst each other so that the old woman could not hear.

"We have to come up with a reason for the old woman to go somewhere other than here. We need this clock to ourselves," whispered Ed.

Unbeknownst to them, the old woman was intensely listening.

She interrupted and said, "Be forewarned."

Melissa stepped closer to the old woman and said, "This clock is a gem. Why do you wish for us never to travel through time?"

"You must hear me out. I am wise and beyond my prime," the old woman said.

"Tell us more. Exactly why?," asked Melissa.

"Are you sure?," asked the old woman.

"Yes," Melissa replied as she and the others nodded.

"Well, you see, a long time ago in my youth, I thought I was in love and wanted to know my own fate too fast. Thus, I moved the clock's hands to future days. I was disappointed by what I discovered. My lover had broken my heart and left. I now dwell alone. There's his picture on the shelf," said the old woman as she pointed to the photo.

Ingrid said, "That is so sad."

The old woman went on to say that during the time of her relationship, she felt anger knowing their fate.

"Please ma'am, would you mind if we were to travel into the future to see what happens to us?," Ingrid asked.

The four teens spent the next hour convincing the old woman that allowing them to travel to the future and past would be grand. Finally, the old woman gave in. She agreed to let the teens experience time travel for themselves since she was unable to convince them otherwise. Tom took control of the clock and gave the hands a spin. Suddenly, it was twenty years later.

Chapter 4

The friends glanced around the funeral home they had stepped into and then looked at one another. Ingrid was nowhere in sight. At a short distance, they witnessed Ingrid's brother in tears.

The friends overheard him saying, "I miss my sister."

Tom, Melissa and Ed had, indeed, landed at Ingrid's funeral twenty years into the future. Melissa suddenly burst out with a loud gasp and formed an enormous smile which seemed inappropriate for a funeral. She had glanced down at her hand, discovering a big diamond ring on her wedding ring finger.

Tom immediately looked in Ed's direction asking, "How could Melissa possibly be happy after discovering Ingrid is dead?"

Ed, however, had no time to answer menial questions. He was in a hurry to venture to other places in time.

"I'd like to travel back to the past when life forms were in the beginning stages. Let's go to prehistoric times!," said Ed with excitement.

Ed grabbed hold of the clock and spun the hands rapidly to where the group of teenagers landed in prehistoric days. Sure enough, the landscape looked deserted with dirt and heavy boulders.

Tom shouted, "Run!," as a dinosaur approached from below. The four friends were temporarily safe on top of a hill. There was a bit of a power struggle between Tom and Ed.

The clock was in Ed's possession, so he knew that there was no need to run. Ed figured that if danger were to come upon them, he could simply move the hands of the clock. He held the power to leave within his hands and found humor in seeing Tom so frightened. Though, the dinosaur was becoming uncomfortably close.

Ed decided the fun was over. He ordered the others to calm down and said that there was no need to run, as though he was coaching them.

Chapter 5

Ingrid took hold of the clock and set the year to 1401. However, the group of teens only spent time there for a split second before Ed regained control of the clock. He changed time to a future year, being eager to study the stock market and winning lottery numbers. They landed in the future one year later than current times.

Ed took notes of the lottery and stock market numbers before the four friends returned to the present. It seemed best to invest in rockets. The teens were able to catch up on their sleep while traveling through time.

As soon as they safely landed back at the old woman's house, an argument erupted. The group was fighting over which years to travel to next. Ed tried to control the situation by saying each one would have a chance to choose. They backed away from one another and regained their composers.

Tom asked, "How about 1985?"

Melissa, Ingrid and Ed agreed that 1985 would be fine. Throughout the entire argument, the old woman stood by. Melissa asked the old woman for her opinion about their situation; however, the old woman remained silent. She had already forewarned them.

Shortly after the situation appeared to have settled down, Tom and Ed broke out in a physical fight over the clock. Tom held time within his hands. Ed backed away and raised his hands as though he was surrendering.

Ed said, "I'm done with time travel. I will win the lottery and score big on the stock market. I'm staying here."

Ed asked Melissa to please stay behind as well.

She replied, "I might," to appease him.

She then turned away from Ed with a sly grin and a devilish wink. Thus, Tom, Ingrid and Melissa traveled to the years they wanted, leaving Ed behind in the present.

The three time travelers were nervous, yet excited. As stated, Tom chose 1985 as their destination. Ingrid picked 1953 and Melissa wanted 2005. They all agreed to the plan.

Ed remained with the old woman. He was on his way to win money and riches. After Tom, Ingrid and Melissa left, Ed and the old woman had a conversation about Ed's short time travel experience. The old woman asked him if he had learned anything from his adventure. Ed replied that after seeing Ingrid's hurst and Melissa's wedding ring, he had, indeed, been taught a lesson.

"Tom and I argued most of the time. The fighting amongst us was a bit turbulent," said Ed.

The old woman was glad that Ed had seen the light and stayed behind.

Chapter 6

Tom, Ingrid and Melissa first took a trip to the past in the year 1953, despite Ed's plea not to go. The 1950's seemed quite grand; although, there was even more inequality than where they came from. The women's liberation era had not yet occurred, as an example. The 1950's were not all peaches and roses.

The three friends took full advantage of their opportunities. They were out for fun. The group had landed in Washington, D.C.; thus, they decided to attend a professional baseball game at Griffith Stadium in hopes of seeing legendary players.

In order to pay for entrance fees, they would need to first earn money. Tom was hired at a movie theater, pretending to be from the 1950's. Ingrid and Melissa got jobs too, as they needed money for room and board. They found a hotel on the avenue to live at temporarily. With money they earned, the three were able to change their appearance to match the era.

Eventually, they had enough money to purchase tickets to see the New York Yankees game. Tom hoped to see Mickey Mantle, especially. He knew baseball inside and out. He was well aware that this game would be amazing.

Melissa and Ingrid knew little about baseball; therefore, Tom taught them as though they were in training while they watched the game. The crowd roared when Mickey Mantel hit a 565-foot home run. Tom was excited as he labeled himself as the "Number One New York Yankees Fan." He could recite all of the statistics. The girls found the game to be interesting; although, they were ready to venture into a different year.

When the game was through, Tom picked up the clock to change the year, but the clock wouldn't tick. That was exactly what the old woman had feared.

Chapter 7

Tom, Ingrid and Melissa were trapped in the year 1953. Melissa nearly had a mental breakdown. The three friends vowed to find a way back to the present. Tom tried to fix the broken clock; but, it was dead. The hands were positioned at six o'clock.

Tom had left his glasses behind. Nevertheless, he was able to see tiny black letters imprinted on the back of the clock as he examined it. The writing told the location where the clock was made. Luck was on their side, or maybe fate, because the clock was made in Washington, D.C. The writing was a bit blurry; however, they were able to read the address. It read, "28495 Sixth Street". They spent the next day traveling there by foot.

Upon their arrival, they found the address to be a jewelry store called, "Sixth Street Jewelers". The three entered the door. The place was old and a bit run down. At the counter was a beautiful woman who said her name was Joanne. There were no other customers in the store.

"What can I do for you?," asked Joanne.

Tom handed her the clock and asked if it could be repaired. Joanne looked as though she was in shock. She was unprepared for this.

"Where did you find this?," Joanne asked with wide opened eyes.

Tom used his wit saying that it had fallen from the sky. Joanne told the teenagers that they must be truthful despite the fact they were strangers to one another.

"I can have the clock fixed today on the condition that you start behaving and begin telling the truth," said Joanne.

The three agreed out of desperation. They told Joanne the story of how they acquired the clock. Joanne knew far more than she would say; however, the clock was fixed that day as promised.

Chapter 8

Tom, Ingrid and Melissa traveled quickly back to present time as soon as the clock had been repaired. The old woman and Ed welcomed the three back. The old woman even had snacks waiting for them.

Ed informed the three friends that he had gotten to know the old woman while they were away. The old woman sat in her chair knitting as she listened. Tom, Ingrid, Melissa and Ed all agreed never to travel through time again. They would let time run its own course. The four friends said it was time to leave the old woman's house, as their ride was there.

Tom, Ingrid and Melissa nearly fell to the floor as Ed said, "Goodbye, you have been more than kind, Joanne."

Tom, Ingrid and Melissa stopped dead in the tracks, temporarily forgetting about the prom.

"What name did you call the woman?," Tom asked Ed.

Ed stated, "Joanne. Why?"

"Because we met Joanne in 1953," replied Tom.

Joanne stepped in and said, "That's right. I am the same woman you met back then."

"Enlighten us some more," said Ed.

Joanne, however, said she wasn't able to say anymore. Thus, the four friends continued on to the prom. By the time they arrived, the prom was near its end, but their lives carried on. The mystery of the clock remained a mystery. For a brief time though, the four friends were able to get a glimpse of the clock's capabilities. They went on with their lives together; although, the mystery of why they were destined to meet the old woman would someday be revealed.

[BOOK II]

Chapter 1

The year was 1953. Joanne was twenty two and worked for a jeweler. Not only did the store sell jewelry, it also sold clocks. Sam, the jeweler, was well liked by everyone. He trained Joanne about the business and taught her how to fix clocks and jewelry.

Every now and then, Sam was visited by a group of men wearing uniforms exhibiting badges. Joanne always wondered why men from the government would occasionally meet with Sam.

One fateful day as Joanne was at work behind the counter, Sam had a massive heart attack and fell dead to the floor. Joanne was left to operate the business on her own. About a month later, before her encounter with Tom, Ingrid and Melissa, another uniformed man from the government entered the store. He asked Joanne if the clock located in the safe had been repaired yet. She was unaware of the clock. Yet, she lied and told him that she was unable to fix the clock since she didn't have access to the safe. To her surprise, the man handed her a red-colored key that would open up this mystery.

Chapter 2

Joanne had been fully aware that Sam had been working on a secret government mission, but she had no knowledge of what it entailed. There were actually two clocks that had the ability to change time to the past and future. Joanne learned of them after opening the safe. She discovered the clocks, spare parts, and documents.

While reading through the paperwork, she became aware of the clocks' powers to time travel. What a discovery she had made! Joanne never let the man from the government know there were two clocks of the same kind. She assumed that Sam had secretly made a duplicate for himself.

After Joanne assured the government man that she would fix the clock, he left. Moments later, a young man, Alex, walked into the store. Joanne's heart dropped and she giggled as he conveyed his love for her. Alex was the man who had truly captured her heart. She was fond of Alex ever since the day they met in their teenage years. He was on temporary leave from the Army and would only be in the area for two months.

Joanne closed up shop during the two month time frame. She spent the months with Alex before he returned to the Army. They both had the time of their lives. Unfortunately, time flew too fast. Alex was leaving. Joanne gave him a hug and kiss just before his plane took off into the darkened sky. He said nothing about ever returning. Joanne's heart was broken. Unlike clocks and jewelry, her heart she could not repair. Over the years, she became soft spoken and lonely.

Chapter 3

Time moved on for Joanne. She never married. Although years later, she fell in love with Simon. He was handsome and an elite member of society. He had been a professional football player until his retirement. Simon was well known within his city and flaunted his wealth. Joanne catered to his every need. She often bought him gifts as well. She would spend days and weeks waiting for Simon to make time for her. Joanne overrated him. She rarely smiled, though she believed she was in love with him.

Eventually, Joanne had enough. She had to know the fate of her relationship with Simon. The clock in her possession tempted her like bait. Joanne moved the clock's hands to future hours. She discovered that Simon had left her as though she meant nothing to him. Because of her time travel, she always owned the knowledge that her relationship would not last. Joanne never quite knew where she belonged.

Chapter 4

The year was 1973. Joanne was forty two. Since Simon was no longer in her life, Joanne spent the next four decades dwelling alone. She thought that she might have still been with Simon had she not seen their fate. One of the two clocks remained in her possession. The government had the other one. She kept the clock so that no one else would ever fall into the clock's deception. Joanne was fully aware of the dangers the clocks held. They possessed empowerment which could easily be misused.

Four decades later, the year was 2015. Joanne was eighty five. She continued to live alone in good health. She rarely left her home and saved every penny she had. Joanne prayed to God that someday He would show her a sign that would lead the way to where she belonged before the end of her time.

[BOOK III]

Chapter 1

Tom, Ingrid, Melissa and Ed had just left for the prom. The old woman, Joanne, shed a tear after they shut the door. She was going to miss their company. Afterward, she sat in deep thought, wondering if they might have been her sign from God. Just then, it hit her like a brick. She realized the teenagers' names spelled out T.I.M.E. (Tom, Ingrid, Melissa, Ed). Everything was beginning to fall into place. Although, most was still a mystery. Joanne did not know the overall purpose for the teenagers' visit.

One day, in 2015, Joanne's doorbell rang. When she opened it, an elderly man was standing on her porch serenading her with a love song. Joanne began to giggle, being fully aware he was Alex! She smiled from ear to ear. The love of her life had found her after all those years.

Chapter 2

Alex and Joanne spent the next few days reminiscing about their teenage years. It was as if both were in a daze each time they looked at one another. Every day together was a celebration. Their hearts could not be happier. Neither one had a good explanation as to why they spent most of the years apart.

Joanne and Alex shared everything about their lives. Joanne even explained all about the clock. Alex assured her that he would never again leave her side.

"We are now together forever," Alex said.

His statement couldn't be more true. They spent eternity traveling back and forth through time. They never feared death because they never traveled that far into the future. The mystery was done. The clock had been placed in Joanne's life for a good reason. It brought the two lovers the opportunity to live without regret. Since Alex and Joanne met in their teenage years, God sent teenagers whose names spelled out T.I.M.E as her sign. The couple lived forever as did their love story.

"Joanne, this was all meant to be," said Alex as small tears of joy fell from his eyes.

Chapter 3

The couple became officially united and danced under the moonlight sky. Joanne and Alex were meant to find one another and live their lives in love for all of time. This was their destiny.

The hands of time is a tale of fate. It is not impossible to reverse the paths we choose to travel if you believe. With God, anything is possible.

THE END

GET A LIFE

A Tale of Gratitude

Chapter 1

Flat broke and homeless, nothing made me happy and no one could make me laugh. I had enough food to eat, but only for a day. My life was a mess.

I wandered down a lonely street, kicking up the autumn leaves. As I strayed into an alley, I came upon an intriguing store. I stepped inside and wanted to explore. Even so, the clerk instructed me to check in and take a seat.

"Wait your turn, ma'am," said the clerk.

I was curious and still unsure what type of store I had entered. One by one, each person waiting was called upon. Moments later, it was my turn. A guide led me down several hallways with many rooms. Each room I passed had a glass window.

As I slowly walked by, I read signs that said, "Give me a try."

Mannequins appeared in each window with descriptions about their life. Each and every mannequin had the inscription, "Get a Life." I asked the guide about this place.

The guide responded, "'Get a Life' is the name of the store. Pick one life just as if you were choosing a hat. Once your choice is made, say the word 'open' at the end of the hallway. A door will then open for you to enter where you will fall. You will land in your new home and begin a brand new life. There is no need to worry. You will not be alone. There will be people who care about you."

Chapter 2

The windows of each room were like glass cases. Every mannequin, whether it was a child, a man, or one of many varied races, was different from one another. Each life had pro's and each life had flaws. Though as previously stated, I could only choose one.

Since I was struggling just to survive, I found joy and excitement at this store. I smiled for the first time since becoming homeless when I made my decision to become a child. The guide instructed me to sign a two-hundred page contract. My age of thirty two would change to ten. I was to be placed in the life of a girl who is clever and has traveled the world. The contract was so long that it nearly made me blind. I was not sure what it said, but I agreed and signed it.

The girl's life that I chose displayed an advertisement that read this: "You can be great like me!"

This was the description by her mannequin:

> "I am a girl, ten years old
> My life is bliss
> With a heart of gold
> My family is rich
> I've traveled the world
> Here is my sales pitch
> I'm a wonderful girl
> I have only one problem
> I may not live to be old
> Although my life is really awesome
> To you it must be sold".

Chapter 3

The sale was finalized.

I walked down the hallway and said the word, "Open."

Suddenly, I fell into my new home. I became a girl named Amber with a loving family. It was interesting that they did not wonder why I was there. It was as if I had always been under their care.

On the inside, I was still myself. I had purchased a life, not a person. It became time to live carefree.

My new mother said, "It's time to go to bed, Amber."

I thought she was joking.

I replied, "It's only eight o'clock."

My mother said, "Yes, eight o'clock is your bedtime."

The bed was comfortable and cozy; however, my mother's orders made me wish I was thirty two again. My new parents had full control of me which made me wonder about the life I was sold.

I went to bed at eight o'clock as I was told, although I was not happy about it. That night, I cried myself to sleep. Luckily, the next day was better. It was Saturday which I was told was my day to play outside.

My mother said, "Don't forget to wear your sweater."

I did not appreciate her telling me constantly what to do. In spite of that, I enjoyed playing with the other kids at the local park that day. By dusk, the kids and I wanted to continue to play; however, our parents called us in for dinner. Previously being homeless, I had lacked for food so having a prepared meal each night became a treat. *I thought to myself, "Being a child is the key."*

Chapter 4

After a while, I became used to my parents and the daily routine. I liked having enough food and a roof over my head. Life was great until the day of my doctor appointment.

My mother approached me and said, "It's three o'clock. It's time to go to the doctor."

I asked, "For my cold sore?"

She replied, "No, it's to check for cancer. You're in remission."

So that must have been the problem that I read about when I was sold this life. Immediately, I began wishing for my old life back even though I had been hungry, lacking food and shelter.

Chapter 5

Upon my return from the doctor, I had great concern. In hast, I thumbed through my agreement. I then took a deep breath and spent time carefully reading the entire two-hundred page contract front and back. It read that Amber may not live a long life. In fine print, the words were, "Give, give, give." On the back of the paperwork was a phone number. Immediately, I called the number. The clerk answered. I informed her that I had made it to my new home safely; however, things were not always so great.

"The contract states that there is a path nearby that leads to a gate where I can enter into my old life. Where exactly is the path?," I asked the clerk as I begged her for my old life back.

The clerk replied, "Give. It will work. Give to those who lack."

She then ended the call.

Chapter 6

I soon gave away my overabundance of toys and money to girls and boys in need. I called the clerk again, although she told me to leave her alone and hung up. Amber's life was not the life I wanted anymore. It is a bit cliche, but you don't know what you have until it's gone. This I was shown. I then knew where I belonged.

Day and night, I prayed to God to lead the way. I wandered aimlessly outside one cold, chilly night. Suddenly, the path I was walking had a gate. I entered upon my old life. Back to being homeless, I felt warmth and happiness inside myself. My life was still a mess, though I had renewed inspiration. I must have been gone for a while because there were Christmas lights for miles.

Chapter 7

I found cardboard and made a sign that read, "My life is a true blessing." I displayed the sign on a street within my hometown. People were handing me gifts and money. In the blink of an eye, a man pulled me aside.

I heard the man say, "I want you as my bride."

When I looked up at his face, I saw the love of my life! He was the only man I had ever fallen in love with. He said he had been searching for me for months.

I agreed to marry him as the crowd applauded. My dreams had all come true. Nothing had been lost. I had gained wisdom by learning that no other life is worth the cost. Christmas bells rang and a crowd sang as we married on Christmas Day.

THE END

MOTHER NATURE'S REVENGE

A Domestic Violence Story

Chapter 1

Have you ever known someone with the power to change the world? Have you known a person who could make others think twice about hitting a woman or girl? Mother Nature is a personification of the forces of nature. She is defined as having some love and said to be caring sometimes. What you don't know, however, is that she is a real person. This will be shown within the tale.

The story begins with the Big Bang. Mother Nature and Father Time had recently married. The reception afterward was so loud, it caused the Big Bang.

The couple began their lives together with love, peace, harmony and happiness. Mother Nature was constantly singing. Over time, Father Time became quite bitter. Suddenly without warning, he loudly chimed as he struck Mother Nature. Yes, you got that right. He struck her with one movement of a hand when they fought. Mother Nature was bruised and battered.

As time carried on, so did the abuse. Father Time misused his power with his brawn. One day, Mother Nature had enough of the violence. She ordered Father Time to pack his things and leave. Thus, the couple divorced. Father Time took his time leaving, but finally rode away on horse. This left Mother Nature free to do as she pleased. She put enjoyment on hold so that she could first attend support groups at a church. Her soul had been scarred.

Mother Nature discovered that she was not alone. There were others in the support groups who had also been abused. It seemed that physical, emotional and mental abuse was far too common. Nearly all members of the groups were women who had been mistreated by men. Mother Nature found this to be a problem. Thus, one cold, damp autumn day, she used her power for revenge.

Chapter 2

The time was five o'clock. Jessica and Austin both woke up to the sound of their alarm clock buzzing. It was the day of the exam and neither one wanted to be late. Austin began the morning by making coffee.

"Are you excited?," asked Jessica.

"Yes, I can't wait to get to the Boston hospital. Today's the day we'll find out if we're having a boy or a girl," replied Austin.

Jessica and Austin were on their way to Jessica's ultrasound appointment. She was pregnant with Austin's baby. The time was then seven o'clock. They had made it to the exam on time.

"Congratulations. You'll be having a baby girl," said the doctor.

Jessica and Austin were filled with excitement and awe. Jessica was the happiest woman in the world. Austin was just as happy as he had been wishing for a girl.

Both Jessica and Austin called family and friends to give them the news. However, Austin was unable to reach his best friend. Later that day, the couple discovered the reason when they saw Austin's best friend on the news for violently beating his girlfriend. It was disturbing to Jessica and Austin that Austin's friend had turned so violent. The couple had no knowledge about domestic violence so they made a pact with one another to study the subject for better comprehension.

As the couple continued to watch the news on television, a banner flashed across the screen that read, "Breaking news". The journalist reported that the world that day witnessed uncountable fights. Women everywhere were being battered and bruised. Men were being arrested and quickly set free as jails were at their maximum capacity. Politicians would have to pass new laws and address this critical issue immediately.

Just then, Jessica got a phone call from her best friend, Sue. She said that she was happy for Jessica and Austin and then announced that she was having a baby girl too. Jessica was excited for her friend and wanted to chat longer; however, Austin nudged her and told her she should get some sleep. Jessica had work in the morning. Austin and Jessica drifted off to sleep and were awoken the next morning as the alarm clock buzzed.

Austin made coffee and stumbled over to turn on the television. "Breaking news" flashed across the screen again. Baby girls were being born all over the world. No boys were being born! People were frantic. Cities blasted emergency horns. The world would, thus, be surrounded by innumerable women and girls.

Chapter 3

Mother Nature can be mean at times, although she was trying to teach the world a lesson. Every minute of each new day only girls were being born. Mother Nature had found a way for revenge from being scorned.

A policeman, Mitch, resigned from his job to focus his time on a mission. He sought to find Mother Nature's undisclosed location so that the world could understand her reasons for causing chaos. Mitch began his investigation while, in the meantime, Austin and Jessica further studied domestic violence. The couple became aware of the Violence Wheel. In the wheel's center is power and control. Abusers use power and control in eight varied ways which are as follows:

- Using coercion and threats
- Using intimidation
- Using emotional abuse
- Using isolation
- Minimizing, denying and blaming
- Using children
- Using male privilege
- Using economic abuse

(If you are a victim of this, you are also a shining star. Your future can still hold happiness. Keep the faith).

Jessica and Austin learned a lot from studying day and night. The couple rarely argued and when they did, it was settled nonviolently. They listened attentively to one another.

While the couple was busy studying and the world was in utter chaos, Mitch was in bliss at the thought of soon becoming famous. He had found Mother Nature's home and invited himself inside. Mitch discovered her all alone. He interviewed Mother Nature for hours. She was a kind woman with a bit of a mean streak. Through talking with her, Mitch learned that she had been mistreated. To make a point, every parent would be greeted with a new baby girl - not a boy!

Mitch tried to negotiate a plan with Mother Nature. The deal was that men would no longer abuse women within their lifespans. When and if there was a change in behavior, Mother Nature would once again allow the birth of baby boys.

Chapter 4

The agreement was finalized. Mitch was certain the outcome from his negotiations with Mother Nature would bring him fame and fortune. Mother Nature insisted that all abuse stop. Mitch claimed he would be persistent about it once he returned to his homeland. Both were satisfied with the deal.

Mitch returned home. He was on a new mission to stop domestic violence. He had great ambition to first educate himself and others. Mitch made thousands of phone calls and was referred to Austin and Jessica. By then, the couple was considered to be experts in the field of domestic violence. They had even become professors.

Mitch explained that he had met with Mother Nature and made an agreement. Men could no longer be so mean. Thus, Jessica and Austin created a foundation to educate the world and save all women and girls. The world stopped to listen. People actually understood. It was as though all humanity had arisen. Men stopped hurting those around them. They were converting to love, not hate.

Following the change in men's behavior, Jessica found out that her second child would be a boy! Other women began experiencing the same news. The world would, thus be saved. There was breaking news all over the world. Radios, televisions, newspapers and the internet reported the birth of both boys and girls. People stared at their televisions in awe. The world was in shock, yet also in its glory. Mother Nature had lived up to her part of the bargain.

Chapter 5

Mother Nature was onto her next lesson. She was a blessing within the world. Although, she only had half a heart. She wanted each person to do their best. Earthquakes, wildfires and such were her way of teaching.

God had the ultimate say of how things would go. When people received blessings, it was based on prayers He had heard. However, that is a different story. This one is nearly finished. The world was in its glory and the pain had diminished. Oh, and by the way, the reason we now say "A**men**" after we pray is so that we never again lose the **men**. Each time "Amen" is said, a new baby boy is born to be loved and adorned.

THE END

A MYSTERIOUS SALESMAN

A Time Travel Tale

Chapter 1

The Meeting

Real estate sales had fallen ever since the pandemic of 2020. Cash was given one last chance at selling homes or ultimately, he would be fired. He had been the lowest ranking salesman of the previous quarter. Thus, his job was on the line.

Cash was a fifty-eight year old heavy-set man with a beard and mustache. He had only been a real estate salesman for one year. Cash wore second-hand suits and ties only because his job required dressing up. Otherwise, he wore t-shirts, jeans, and boots.

Cash had been a factory laborer throughout his entire career until the plant shut down. He was out of work for two years applying for jobs every week with no luck. Holden, the real estate company owner, took a chance on hiring Cash after a recommendation from his cousin, Isaac. Cash and Isaac were old acquaintances from the factory.

"Listen, I'm going to help you out. There's several properties that need selling. I've been waiting for the right salesman to hand them over to, and I believe you, Cash, are the right one," said Holden.

Cash was ever grateful. Holden handed him the list of properties, including a list of potential buyers.

"Thank you, thank you so much," Cash said.

"You came highly recommended by my cousin. I can't let family down," Holden replied.

After Cash left his office, Holden immediately placed a call to the president of his real estate company, Ben Scholar.

"Haha, I am finally going to be able to let go of the Birmingham Properties. I found the perfect salesman for the job. I've got Cash in charge," Holden said with a chuckle and sigh of relief.

"Do you think he is really capable?," asked Ben.

"I can't think of a better sucker for the job," said Holden.

Ben felt a sense of relief as well. The Birmingham Properties had been for sale for ten years; however none of the salesmen would accept the task of selling them. They knew the secret those properties held. Cash, however, had been left in the dark.

Chapter 2

The Erickson Family

The summer sun warmed the country air as Cash took the lead in his rusty old pick-up truck. He was heading to the first property to show. Following behind was the Erickson family, consisting of Millard, his wife Ruth, and their two children, Bobby and Elon. Their two-story house had caught on fire and was unsalvageable. Everyone made it out safely; however, they were left to seek temporary housing with Ruth's aunt and uncle.

The family had previously visited numerous properties with a different realty company. Being especially dissatisfied with the realtor, Millard switched to Holden Realties. He seemed pleased with his decision after a lengthy phone conversation with Holden. Although, he still appeared a bit cautious.

Corn fields surrounded the old country road as the two vehicles pulled into a prodigious, well-maintained farm house. The Erickson family's eyes all lit up at the amazing sight. Millard asked how much of the land was included.

Cash answered, "Forty acres."

Ruth turned in Millard's direction with excitement. She had always dreamed of having land for horses.

Cash gave his best sales speech before everyone entered the home. He highlighted the land, once again, and the recent upgrades and maintenance. He included the fact that the house was completely furnished and the below market price. Cash informed the Erickson's that the house was built in 1958 and that it included a fallout shelter. He added that the installation of fallout shelters was increasingly popular around that era.

Millard was a longtime grocery store manager and; therefore, he was fairly business savvy. He was a bit suspicious at the low cost of the property. His assumption was that there had to be something wrong. Without saying so, Millard was set on hiring a building inspector before making any purchases.

Upon entering the house, Bobby and Elon were in awe. The two boys immediately darted over to the enormous flat screen television remote. There was even a gaming system attached to the T.V. Millard and Ruth could not believe the high quality of the decorations and furniture. Ruth said it felt like home and Millard was in agreement. There was a warm and cozy feeling inside the house.

The kitchen had all the necessary appliances, including a dishwasher. The room was so large that there was even an island countertop. The four-bedroom house was perfect for their family size. Bobby and Elon would both have their own rooms. Additionally, Millard and Ruth would have the opportunity to decide if they wanted to have one more child. Ruth had really wanted to have a baby girl someday. Although, she had previously stated that as long as she had a healthy baby, she would feel blessed.

Off to the left side of the front of the house was a screened-in porch. In the backyard of the house was a large deck with enough space for a swimming pool. The closest neighbor lived about half a mile down the road.

Millard searched the entire premises, but he was unable to find anything wrong with the property. He and Ruth talked it over with one another. They agreed on purchasing the house after a building inspector examined it. One week later, a leaky faucet was the only problem the inspector could find. The Erickson's were prepared to buy the home.

Chapter 3

Home Purchase

It was the day to close the deal. Besides having insurance money from the fire, Millard had a fairly large savings and investment account. His stingy, penny pinching had really paid off. Holden informed Millard that there was no need for him to hire a lawyer since the Erickson's would not have a mortgage. They were paying in full with cash. Millard saw that as more money in his pocket, not having to pay for legal services.

The Holden Realty company lawyer, Jack Ellington, drew up the purchase agreement. The papers appeared as large as a book. The meeting consisted of Jack, Holden, Millard and Ruth. Holden distracted the Erickson's with small talk as Jack talked quickly about each paper they were signing. However, he talked so fast that he slipped one page for signatures without Millard and Ruth realizing it. Holden and Jack's plan was successful. Holden was to converse with the Erickson's while Jack used quick smooth talk. The deal was done.

"Congratulations Mr. and Mrs. Erickson," Holden said.

"Thank you," replied Millard and Ruth.

"I believe you will be more than pleased with your purchase. And as well, you did our company a favor. Ever since the pandemic, it has been a tough business selling homes. Again, congratulations. Here are the keys to your new home. Move in anytime you like. The property is yours," said Holden.

Millard and Ruth walked out of the meeting room with hope for the future. They felt they had found the deal of a lifetime. The couple drove away to their temporary house to give the good news to their sons. Bobby and Elon were elated. As well, Ruth's aunt and uncle were happy for them and also happy for themselves. There had been some tension in the household with four added people. Ruth's aunt and uncle owned a rather small house which barely had enough room for the additional guests.

A new house and a new life were about to begin for the Erickson family. They all helped to pack the car and headed to the country. As they approached the house, excitement filled their eyes. Millard pulled into the driveway. When he stopped the car, he watched as Ruth, Bobby and Elon ran to the front door. Although, they had to wait for Millard so that he could open it with his new keys.

Chapter 4

The Erickson's New Home

Millard unlocked the front door and the family of four stepped inside their new home. They witnessed an entirely different interior. As each one starred in disbelief, the door shut suddenly on its own.

"This place looks like something out of the 1950's!," exclaimed Ruth.

"Where's the gaming system? And where's the big screen T.V.?," hollered Bobby.

"I don't know, son," replied Millard, still in a state of shock.

Millard, Ruth, Bobby and Elon each went their separate ways as they explored the home. The furniture, the appliances, the television, and pictures on the wall did, indeed, appear to derive from the 1950's era.

"Where's the T.V. remote? I can't find it?," Bobby said in panic.

"It appears we've been scammed. Let me make a phone call," said Millard to his family.

Millard had left his mobile phone inside his car. Opening the door, he stepped onto a newspaper lying on the front step. Not thinking anything of it, he began to walk towards his car and discovered it was no longer in the driveway. Instead, a 1956 Chevrolet Bel Air was parked there.

Millard became a little frightened by the thought that someone had stolen his car. He feared that a stranger was nearby. Millard immediately headed to the front door to ensure the safety of his family. Without much thought, he picked up the newspaper, entered the door, and placed the paper on the coffee table. Ruth and the boys were in the living room with the television on. There were only three stations and every show was in black and white.

"Did you call Cash?," Ruth asked Millard.

"It seems that someone is playing a prank on us. My car is missing, meaning my phone is missing as well," Millard stated as he tried to appear calm and collected.

"Which means my phone is gone too," Ruth said.

"Oh no, don't tell me you left your phone in the car too?," Millard asked with great concern.

"Unfortunately, yes I did," she replied.

"Okay, well I'm going around the house inside and out to make sure things are safe. Stay here with the boys while I check the perimeters," Millard instructed Ruth.

As Millard entered Elon's bedroom, he picked up a baseball bat for protection. He examined every room, every closet, the basement and the outside. Millard could not find anyone.

In the meantime, Ruth picked up the newspaper lying on the coffee table while the boys watched television. In only a matter of a minute, she realized the newspaper was dated July 15, 1958. Startled, she threw the paper down and her heart rate increased. Millard then entered the room, stating that no one was on the property. He went ahead to inform Ruth that a vintage car was in the driveway with keys in the ignition.

"Who could it belong to?," Ruth asked Millard.

"I haven't got a clue, but as I said, I looked in every corner of the house and everywhere on the property. There isn't a soul in sight but us," he said.

Ruth informed Millard that the television shows were all reruns from the 1950's. Just then, the evening news aired for July 15, 1958, including footage of President Dwight D. Eisenhower. Millard and Ruth looked into one another's eyes and both said the same thing. They wondered if they had traveled back in time.

"What year did Cash say this house was built?," Ruth asked her husband.

"1958," replied Millard with an expression of awe.

The Erickson family was growing tired and hungry. They decided to accept their situation for the remainder of the night with plans to venture out the following day. In the meantime, Ruth prepared dinner with a fully stocked refrigerator and freezer. Shortly after finishing their meals, the family retired for the night to their bedrooms.

Chapter 5

The Gibson Family

The season was the Summer of the current year. Cash was driving his pick-up truck to the store when Holden called.

"Another deal is completed. Cash, you're doing a fine job selling these properties. Keep it going and you could earn employee of the year," Holden said.

"Thank you," Cash replied.

"The Gibson family is all set. I handed them the keys to their new home, built in 1895, literally minutes ago. By the way, you haven't received any complaint calls from the Erickson family I presume, correct?," Holden asked.

"I haven't heard a word. That is correct," said Cash.

"Excellent, excellent," replied Holden.

The call between Holden and Cash ended, and Cash continued his journey to the store. In the meantime, the Gibson family was on the way to their newly purchased house. Allen, his wife Maya, and their children, Elizabeth, Naomi, and Daniel comprised the Gibson family. Like the Erickson family, the Gibson's purchased a fully furnished home.

Allen had recently won a large sum of money playing the lottery. Thus, the family wished to upgrade from a mobile home with worn out, second-hand furniture. The 1895 colonial style house with modern furniture and decorations was more than they dreamed.

The house was painted yellow with a white trimmed front porch. It was located in the middle of a neighborhood surrounded by similar houses. Maya thought it was the perfect place to further raise her family. There would be plenty of other children for Elizabeth, Naomi, and Daniel to form friendships.

Since the homes were built in the nineteenth century, people parked their cars along the street, as there were no driveways. It was mid afternoon when Maya pulled up in front of the house and parallel parked the car. The Gibson family rushed out of the car. The kids then began running around and doing cartwheels on their new property.

"Come on, kids. Let's go inside," shouted Allen.

After the Gibson's were all inside, the door shut behind them, just as it happened to the Erickson family. The rooms' only light came from the windows. Allen searched for the light switches, but could not find any. Maya and the kids were stunned to see wood furniture, antique artwork and other old items instead of the modern furniture they had last seen.

"Did we enter the wrong house?," Maya asked Allen.

"It appears so. Let me go check the house number," he replied.

As soon as Allen opened the door, he had another surprise. Horses and buggies passed by on the brick-laid road. Furthermore, there were no cars parked along the street. Just then, Naomi came outside.

"Daddy, I have to go to the bathroom. I can't find it inside," said Naomi.

"Tell your mother to come outside. She'll have to take you into the woods. In fact, have everyone come outside," replied Allen as he stood both in shock and disbelief.

Maya, Elizabeth and Daniel stepped outside. They also could not believe their eyes.

"I don't like the feel of this," said Maya to Allen.

"Look mommy! Horses!," shouted Daniel.

"Come on. We're going out back. Naomi needs to do her business. I want all of us to stick together," Allen instructed the family.

As the family approached the back of the house, Allen spotted an outhouse. Maya took Naomi inside it as she had never seen an outhouse before. Suddenly the man next door, Sherwin Smith, shouted from his window.

"What kind of clothing is that?," asked the neighbor, Sherwin.

Allen had no response except to tell his family to follow him to the front of the house. To his amazement, neighbors were gathered on the brick road, staring at the Gibson family's attire. They appeared in awe.

"Come on family. Let's hurry and get inside," Allen forcefully instructed.

Once they re-entered the home and shut the door, each family member let out a sigh.

"I think they're after us," Daniel said to his father.

"Not now, son. Maya, do you know how to sew? We need different clothes and we need them now," said Allen.

"I know a little bit about sewing. Not a lot," she responded.

"I'll help you find what you'll need. Kids, behave for a while," said Allen.

A few days passed by. As it turned out, Maya did not need to sew clothing to match the style of the era they had presumably entered. Instead, the family discovered clothes in each bedroom closet. They found food in the home as well.

"This is a nightmare. Now what?" asked Maya to Allen.

"We find a horse and buggy and we ride into town, find Cash, and get this mystery solved," he replied.

Chapter 6

The Ortiz Family

The Summer sun brightly shined down as the Ortiz family ventured to their newly purchased house. Cash had been the realtor who sold them on a 1976 built ranch-style home. The Ortiz family consisted of Mateo, his wife Amelia, and their one daughter, Emery.

Again, like the Erickson's and the Gibson's, the house that the Ortiz family bought that day had been fully furnished. Mateo and Ameilia were a young couple. Emery was merely a toddler. They had been living with Ameilia's parents until they could afford their own place. The price of their first house was more than reasonable. The low cost exceeded their expectations.

Mateo drove a 2020 Ford Escape. Although it was not his dream car, he was satisfied. The car got him from Point A to Point B without problems. Mateo worked in the auto parts department of a Ford dealership. He snagged a great deal on his Ford Escape.

As the family pulled up near the house and into the driveway, Ameilia expressed gratitude and glory. The house had been well maintained and was the perfect size for their small family.

While Amelia was busy getting Emery out of the car, Mateo did not hesitate to enter the home. Before Amelia and Emery had time to get inside, Mateo stepped outside to check the house number. Sure enough, it was 187, which was the right house number.

"You look like you've seen a ghost," Ameila exclaimed.

"Honey, did I drive down the wrong street?," asked Mateo.

"No. This is Vintage Lane. I'm sure of it. What's wrong, Mateo?," asked Amelia.

"Come inside and see for yourself," he said.

When Amelia and Emery stepped inside, it looked nothing like what Cash had shown them. Previously, the house was furnished and decorated with the most up-to-date upholstery and artwork. What the Ortiz family viewed now was pea green shag carpets, a yellow refrigerator, and a green rotary dial wall phone. The entire home appeared to be furnished and decorated in 1970-era style.

As the couple was perusing the house, the front door shut on its own.

"This is completely unacceptable. Do you happen to have Cash's phone number on you?," asked Mateo to Amelia.

"No. The number is in your address book in the glove compartment in your car," informed Amelia.

"I'll be right back," said Mateo as he opened the door and walked outside.

To his surprise, his 2020 Ford Escape had been replaced with a 1975 Ford Pinto.

"Where the heck is my car!," Mateo shouted loud enough for Amelia to hear him from inside.

Amelia immediately picked up Emery and brought her outside.

"My car! It's gone!," exclaimed Mateo to Amelia.

"Um, Mateo darling, take a look at every car passing by. They're all vintage cars," said Amelia.

All of a sudden, people with lawn chairs started lining the street as though they were waiting for something to occur. Amelia had a strong personality. She was brave enough to ask a lady neighbor what was happening. She was told that the 1976 Bicentennial Parade was about to begin.

"What did she say?" Mateo asked Amelia.

"She said it was the 1976 Bicentennial Parade. Isn't that celebrating 200 years of the United States? Why would they be having a parade about it now?" Amelia questioned.

"Because, Amelia, either Cash is playing one heck of a joke on us, or we have found ourselves in a time warp," said Mateo.

Chapter 7

Conclusion

The Erickson, Gibson, and Ortiz families all arrived at 22 Main Street, at one o'clock on July 16, to file a complaint. The only distinction was that each family was in the year that their home was built. The Erickson's were in 1958, the Gibson's were in 1895, and the Ortiz family was in 1976. Holden Realties, located at 22 Main Street, had not opened for business until the year 2004.

Could it be these three families had time traveled from the current year to the past? Or perhaps, they had originally traveled to the future and were destined to return to where they belonged. One will never know as Cash, a mysterious salesman, was unable to be reached.

THE END

THE DISAPPEARANCE OF EVE

A Magical Time Travel Romance

Chapter 1

Introduction

Ladies and Gentlemen, I am about to provide you with the most amazing magic show secret ever told. It is about my boss, Maverick the Magician, and his assistants Jacob, Weston, Camilia and me. My name is Eve. I must tell the secret by sharing a true story. It goes like this.

Maverick and his four assistants traveled town to town, city to city, and state to state, performing shows throughout the year. Maverick was one of the most underrated magicians ever in existence. His performances used more than illusion and sleight of hand. I don't know how he did it, but Maverick was able to perform the Disappearing Act like no one else.

I am not the best at keeping secrets, so I'll let you in on it up front. Maverick the Magician sent his assistants time traveling during the disappearance performance! It was pure magic. Magic is real, I tell you. I know this first hand because I, too, traveled through in time. More impressive than that, though, was the magic of love which I found along my journey.

Let me begin with the story of Jacob's experience. It is fascinating and factual. Although, he has told me that he's glad to be back in current time. Jacob traveled centuries to the past.

Chapter 2

Jacob's Background

Jacob was merely twenty-two years of age. He had worked for Maverick for two years. Maverick was somewhat considered to be Jacob's mentor. Jacob had been interested in magic since he was a young boy. He saved every penny he earned from mowing lawns to purchase his first magic kit. He performed tricks on his friends, family and neighborhood kids. He was actually amazingly talented.

When it came time to apply for college, Jacob gave his parents news they had never expected. He informed them that he was going to become a magician. Jacob's father became distraught and sarcastically laughed at his plan. He sternly told his son that he was to attend college. Jacob and his father were in complete disagreement. Although, after lengthy conversations about the matter, they reached a compromise. Jacob would attend a two-year college, graduate and then be free to decide his future.

During his college years, Jacob was certain he still wanted to be a magician. He performed tricks on his classmates once in a while. However, he had to buckle down and spend most of his time studying if he was to graduate. His hard work paid off as he had graduated with honors nonetheless.

Having the desire to be a magician, Jacob needed assistance. Therefore, he researched schools of magic. Though, instead of applying to the schools, he used smooth talk on the dean of The School of Enchantment. The dean, a magician himself, was more than impressed with Jacob's personality and persistence.

The dean had recently been in contact with Maverick, an old acquaintance. Maverick had expressed a need for an assistant. He asked the dean if he had a recommendation, possibly one of the school's outstanding students. None of the school's students outshined another. The dean informed Maverick that he would keep his eyes and ears open. Jacob was the young man the dean had been waiting for. After the dean met Jacob, he introduced him to Maverick. Days later, Maverick signed Jacob on.

Chapter 3

Jacob's Experience

Maverick and his assistants traveled to each performance in a tour bus that read, "Maverick the Magician", in fancy lettering. We stopped for a show in New York City which was where Jacob was scheduled to assist. Each assistant worked different shows.

Maverick performed his show at a small venue in Manhattan. He began with card tricks using audience participation. Like always, they were amazed by his sleight of hand. He went on to perform other various tricks before the Disappearing Act. Typically, his assistant stepped into a box, escaped through a secret passage, waited backstage, and then returned. This time, however, Maverick tried a new technique. Jacob was about to travel back in time.

"I will now perform the amazing Disappearing Act for you, ladies and gentlemen. My assistant, Jacob the Magnificent, will step inside this box," said Maverick.

Jacob stepped inside and Maverick said the magic words.

"Abracadabra, disappear," he said as he waved a curtain in front of Jacob.

Maverick reopened the curtain, and Jacob was nowhere in sight. Maverick told the audience that he would bring Jacob back by the end of the show. In the meantime, he went on to perform other tricks.

Jacob had disappeared into the year 1892. He found himself traveling third class on board a steamship right before it docked at the Hudson River pier. Third class passengers traveled in crowded and often unsanitary conditions. Jacob was presumed to be an immigrant. First and second class passengers passed through Customs at the pier. However, since he rode third class, Jacob was transferred to a ferry which traveled to Ellis Island. That was where he had to undergo a medical and legal inspection.

The magic show was nearing its end, and it was time to bring Jacob back. No one in the audience knew where Jacob had disappeared to. Even Jacob was unaware beforehand that he would be time traveling. As luck would have it, Jacob was brought out of the past and into current times right before he was to undergo an inspection. He was fortunate because he had no identification with him on Ellis Island.

The audience was in awe at Jacob's return. He had been missing for almost the entire show. Maverick spoke into the microphone, asking Jacob to describe where he had been. When his answer was "Ellis Island", the audience laughed in disbelief. Maverick, however, knew the truth.

Chapter 4

Weston's Background

Weston's background is quite different from Jacob's qualifications and experience. Weston suffers from Autism. Those who met him were unaware of his condition. Only people who were close to Weston could see symptoms. His parents enrolled him in a school for learning disabilities. This was before he was diagnosed and treated. Weston is now thirty-seven years old. Maverick took him under his belt, as Weston had always displayed an interest in magic.

Weston is charming and handsome. He was introduced to Maverick at age twenty-six. At that time, Weston was living in a group home for people with disabilities. He performed magic tricks for the other residents of the home on a daily basis. Wanting to encourage his talent, one of the care workers reached out to the Magicians Association to ask for advice and guidance. Maverick learned of Weston and immediately made contact. He visited the group home, and Weston and Maverick made an instant connection. Maverick taught him several magic tricks.

Maverick hadn't initially intended on hiring Weston. However, after knowing him and his parents for about a year, he brought Weston on board as an assistant. Weston only performs in a show now and then; yet, he travels from place to place with us on a routine basis.

There were times when I wished I was lucky enough to be Weston's girlfriend. However, our other assistant, Camila, snatched him up before I did. Maverick had originally made it a rule that there would be no dating or relationships formed between his staff. He eased up on that, though, after realizing that Weston and Camila made a lovely couple.

CHAPTER 5

Weston's Experience

Like the rest of us, Weston was unaware that Maverick had learned a new technique for the Disappearance Act. And like the audience, none of us believed Jacob when he said he traveled back in time either. Weston was a nonbeliever until it happened to him as well.

While performing on a Friday evening in Andover, Massachusetts, Weston played his role at assisting Maverick. The audience consisted of approximately fifty people. It was a rather small gathering in comparison to most performances.

One cue, Weston stepped inside the box, Maverick waved the curtain over him and said the magic words. In an instant, Weston was gone. He had been sent to the past, specifically the year 1925.

Weston was in the midst of the Roaring Twenties. The name derived from economic growth in the United States. This was driven by recovery from the devastation of World War I. It was also named the Roaring Twenties because of a boom in construction and fast-paced growth of consumer goods such as automobiles and electricity in North America.

Towards the end of Maverick's performance, Weston was brought back to the current day. The audience was baffled. Maverick asked Weston to speak into the microphone and let the audience know where he had been. To everyone's surprise, Weston told of being in Chicago in 1925, and meeting none other than Al Capone himself!

Al Capone was a Chicago gangster who participated in driving the liquor sales underground during Prohibition. He reportedly had 1,000 gunmen and half of the Chicago police force on his payroll.

Nonetheless, the audience was in disbelief. And frankly, so was I. My thoughts were that Jacob and Weston had teamed up to play a joke on everyone. Maverick, however, appeared proud of his accomplishment to send Jacob and Weston back to the past. Camila and I made an agreement. If we, too, were sent to the past, we would believe in Maverick's time travel secret trick. In the meantime, the audience just thought it was part of a comedy routine of the entire performance.

CHAPTER 6

Camila's Background

Camila was a beautiful woman, thirty-five years of age. She was closer in age to Weston than I was, so I understood why they became a couple. Camila stood five feet, ten inches tall, thin, and had long brown wavy hair. Maverick used Camila for his assistant at the more popular shows. When I was first hired, I thought Camila had probably been hired solely for her beauty. However, after I got to know her, I realized that she had the intellect of a scientist. She was actually a near genius in my opinion. Camila and I became best friends.

I learned that Camila's parents performed for the circus. She grew her love for show business through watching them. Her parents were part of the high wire act. At an early age, Camila's parents attempted to train her on the high wire as well. They were, however, unsuccessful as Camila had a fear of heights that she never outgrew. Tragically, her father fell during a performance and was nearly paralyzed. He suffered a severe head injury which left him unable to speak. Still having a desire for show business, Camila opted for magic shows. She felt that the risk for injury was far less than high wire walking.

Having some of the same acquaintances as her parents, Maverick was introduced to Camila. He found her to be beautiful and intelligent which was perfect for his magic shows. Maverick hired her on as an assistant when she was twenty-five years old.

Every so often, Camila's parents make an effort to attend a show. They travel quite far at times and make a vacation out of it. Her parents were proud of her decision to join the entertainment world.

Chapter 7

Camila's Experience

"Ladies and Gentlemen, I am proud to introduce to you, the amazing and talented entertainer of all times, Maverick the Magician," said the Master of Ceremonies.

Maverick and Camila stood smiling on stage as the curtains drew open. Maverick wore a black tuxedo with a black bowtie, while Camila shined in a sparkling, skin-tight long gown. Maverick had rearranged the order of his magic tricks. The Disappearing Act was to be performed first.

Maverick spoke to the audience as Camila stepped inside the box. He then waved the curtain over her and, suddenly Camila disappeared. I expected to see her backstage as I always had during this act. However, Camila had vanished from there too. The thought that she had traveled back in time had not occurred to me since I was a nonbeliever in time travel. Yet upon her return on stage, she told of entering the City of Baltimore in the year 1944. Camila was my best friend. It was difficult not to believe her.

Camila found herself working in a factory alongside men who were terrified of women in the workplace. Because of World War II occurring during this timeframe, hundreds of thousands of men traveled overseas to fight. This left a gap in the workforce; therefore, American executives realized their only solution was to hire women. Before the war, women in the workplace were scarce.

Women made up sixty-five percent of employees in the aircraft industry alone. Though, they faced significant inequality. Skilled female workers made an average of $31.21 per week while men made approximately $54.65.

At the end of the show, Maverick waved the curtain, said the magic words, and Camila reappeared. Upon her return, she spoke into the microphone thanking Maverick for being a kind and generous boss. It wasn't until later that she explained to me that her time working amongst men in 1944 was undignified and distressing. She had personally been harrassed in the workplace. Fortunately enough for her, Camila's stay in 1944 was brief.

I was still a bit skeptical about the time travel journeys which my coworkers were intent on. Camila was my best friend, though. I knew her well enough to know that she didn't lie. I would, however, need to discover the truth first hand.

Chapter 8

Eve's Background

As stated earlier, my name is Eve. I was twenty-seven when I was hired to work for Maverick the Magician. I had been searching for several months for a job after being fired from my previous one. I had been a first-time waitress and had a few mishaps. I spilled hot coffee on the suit of a high-level executive and a drink on a headstrong woman. Neither of them were too friendly about the situations. They both reported the incidences to my manager who, in turn, gave me a warning. The last straw was when I tallied up my customers' tab and forgot to add in the desserts that they had ordered. I was sent out the door that same evening.

I worked harder at finding a job than I did when I actually had a job. I applied for job advertisements, brought my resume in person to businesses, and asked friends and family for job leads. I was about to lose all hope until the day I got a call from Maverick. I had responded to his assistant job advertisement in desperation. I never expected to get a reply. To my surprise, he invited me in for an interview.

The following day, I entered his office and answered his many various questions. First, he asked me to describe my personal background. I explained that I had grown up in the area, graduated high school, and dropped out of college after only one semester. I had plans to be married and raise children instead of gaining an education and entering the workforce. My every dream came to a complete halt the day I walked in on my fiance with another woman. I spent years in a state of depression and despair.

I had menial jobs before becoming a waitress. As well, I lived with my parents until that time. I was proud to be a waitress and actually liked my job. The day I was fired, I walked through the restaurant crying as I approached the exit.

I wasn't sure if Maverick had intended for me to share all of that information. Although, he later told me he appreciated my openness and honesty. Maverick seemed to like my "never be defeated" personality and offered me an assistant position. I gratefully accepted the offer. My life was about to take a spin with a few twists and turns.

CHAPTER 9

The Disappearance of Eve

Camila and I had placed a bet that if I, too, traveled back in time, I owed her five hundred dollars. I had no doubt that time travel did not exist. I still assumed my coworkers might be playing a prank on me. I was sure to win the money.

I decided to use my wit and question Maverick before my next scheduled performance. I asked him if I would time travel as the other assistants claimed had happened to them. Maverick, whom I completely trusted, assured me that I would, indeed, time travel. All of my doubts were beginning to unfold.

I began to wonder where I would be sent for the forty-five minutes I was to disappear. I might travel to medieval times, the renaissance, or even biblical times. It was a mystery to me; however, it was part of my job. And I wasn't willing to walk away from my golden opportunity.

The stage was set. The Master of Ceremonies gave his introductions and the curtains opened. Maverick was wearing his typical black tuxedo and I wore a shimmering mini dress that offset his sparkling bowtie. Again, Maverick performed the Disappearing Act first. I stepped inside the box, he waved the curtain over me and said the magic words. Suddenly, I was in a world of enchantment and disbelief. By the end of the show, Maverick was unable to bring me back!

Chapter 10

The World of What Could Be

I found myself in a future year in the World of What Could Be. Sitting on a park bench with a cool warm breeze blowing across me, I was dazed watching children flying kites. As I tilted my head upward, I saw men, women, and children riding bikes in the bright blue sky. Drones delivering packages flew higher in the distance. I knew then that I had traveled to the future, but I still did not know where.

"Excuse me, ma'am. Could you please tell me where this location is?," I asked the old lady sitting near me.

"Why of course, dear. This is the World of What Could Be. It is where magic comes to life. There are no frowns here. It is an easy-going lifestyle. No cares, no worries, just good old plain enjoyment of life," she said to me.

"So I've landed in a world of make believe," I stated as factual.

"No dear. As I said, this is the World of What Could Be. The future world that could exist based on decisions made in the past," she said.

The old lady gave me food for thought. The decisions not only I make, but everyone else as well, really do pave the path to outcomes. Choices regarding climate change, wars, cures for diseases, and so on, are important as they affect future results.

"And how about adding love to the list?," said a familiar voice.

I was stunned to see Jacob standing right in front of the park bench. I realized I must have been talking to myself.

"Maverick sent you here as well?," I asked Jacob.

"Only at my request. He's having some difficulty bringing you back to the current day. I offered to look for you," he said with a cute boyish grin.

"Is he going to have problems getting you back there too?," I asked.

"I'm not worried. I missed you, Eve. Believe it or not, you've been gone for three weeks. I have cried every night. It's made me realize how much you mean to me," said Jacob.

"I only just arrived here. Three weeks? Really?," I asked.

"Time moves differently during time travel," he replied.

The true secret of this story is that I had forever had a crush on Jacob. I was thrilled to have him here with me in the future. Since Maverick had not yet brought either one of us back, Jacob and I decided to explore the future world.

CHAPTER 11

Love on the Horizon

Venturing through the World of What Could Be, Jacob and I talked and laughed through the park and into a small town. We stopped inside an empty cafe for a bite to eat. A few minutes after sitting down at our table, a robot waitress handed us menus. At first, I found it to be rather odd, but Samantha the robot turned out to be quite humorous. She started off with a couple of jokes which had us laughing out tears. She then gave us time to look over the menus.

Upon Samantha's return, she asked us if we had made our decisions. We ordered our food; however, the robot then asked us what our song choice was. Jacob and I looked at one another in confusion. The robot informed us that she was also a jukebox!

"Obviously, you did not see the back of the menus. There are various songs to choose from which you listen to as you eat. Please make your selection," said Samantha.

Jacob turned toward me and said, "Allow me to select please, Eve."

"Of course, that would be fine," I said.

Jacob and I sat in awkward silence for a couple of minutes until the first song began playing. It made me smile as it was my favorite love song. Jacob then reached out his hands from across the table to hold mine.

"I knew this was your favorite love song," he said.

"How did you know?, I asked him.

"I have a keen sense of hearing. You were telling Camila one day before a performance. I have had a crush on you since your first day of work. I wanted to know everything about you, but I had been too shy to tell you how I felt," said Jacob.

"Too shy? You're never shy," I added.

"Around you, I seem to be. That's a good thing, Eve. It means I like you," he said with a wink.

"Well, I really like you too," I said with joy.

Our meals were ready and served to us. Relaxing piano music played as we ate. After we were done eating and paying the bill, I asked Jacob if he was ready to leave.

"I just have one more surprise," he said.

Just then, Samantha returned with a violin in her robotic hands. She played a beautiful love tune as we sat holding hands and smiling at one another. When the robot was done, she told us to enjoy the rest of our day.

I said, "Thank you," even though I still felt a bit awkward thanking a robot.

Walking down the sidewalks through town, I told Jacob that I just had one question for him.

"How did you slip that one by me? How did Samantha know to play her violin for us and you knew about it beforehand?," I asked.

"Sleight of hand. Are you forgetting I'm in training to become a magician?," he replied.

"I had better keep a good eye on you," I said as we both laughed.

The day couldn't be any brighter. We were both having the time of our lives. And, we were both falling in love.

Chapter 12

The Bleeding Heart

As the sun was setting, Jacob led the way up to a small grassy hill. He somehow made a blanket appear which we sat down on to gaze at the stars. As the evening grew into night, Jacob and I pointed out constellations, counted the stars, and found the brightest one.

"Make a wish," he said.

I kept it to myself. Though my wish was for Jacob and I to, one day, tell the story of our everlasting romance.

"Did you wish?," he asked.

"Yes, did you?," I replied.

"Yes, and if you say you love me as I love you, it will come true," he surprisingly said.

I paused in disbelief momentarily. I felt as though I was in a daze.

"I love you Jacob," I said.

"Ah, so wishes do come true. I love you too, Eve," he said with dreamy eyes.

We then had our first kiss. Although, I was a bit baffled by his next question at first.

"Do you remember the path we took to get here?," asked Jacob.

"Yeah, you just walk that way down the hill and straight into town. Why are you asking me if I know the directions out of here?," I asked.

"In case Maverick is able to bring me back to the current year before you," he informed me.

I hadn't thought about the possibility of that occurring. He must have had a premonition because suddenly it happened. Jacob had vanished!

Chapter 13

Eve's Return

Being absorbed in the moment, I did not realize I had hundreds of mosquito bites. I was only aware of it after Jacob disappeared. I was left to march down the hill and wander aimlessly into the street lit town. After picking up the blanket, I began my journey when, suddenly I was face to face with Maverick! As I gazed at my surroundings, sure enough, I was back to current times!

"Welcome back, Eve," Maverick said.

"I can't thank you enough!," I said with excitement.

"I'm sorry it took so long. It was the first time I sent anyone to the future," he said.

"What happened to the performance after I vanished and didn't come back?," I asked.

"Well, the audience was naturally disappointed. My reviews have fallen. There haven't been as many people at my shows," he stated.

"Oh, I'm sorry to hear that," I said with sincerity.

Maverick went on to say, "We are all just glad to have you back."

Being curious, I asked, "What city or town are we in now?"

"The City of New Orleans," he informed me.

Maverick finished by saying that we were wrapping it up. The show in New Orleans would be our last. He said he was sorry to be giving me the news on such short notice. He added that he would gladly be a reference for me in my job search. Maverick was retiring.

I was shocked to say the least. *Though, the show must go on, I thought.* I wandered backstage before the last performance. Sitting in a chair talking to Weston and Camila sat Jacob. I decided to approach them and include myself in on their conversation. We talked as we always had. Nothing had changed. *I wondered to myself, "Does Jacob even remember anything that had happened. Or had I just been in a dream world?"*

CHAPTER 14

Conclusion

The last magic show concluded in New Orleans. Weston and Camila decided to stay behind and give themselves a much needed vacation. Maverick went his separate way as well. I was saddened that Jacob appeared to have no memory of our time in the future together.

"Where are you heading?," I asked Jacob.

"I thought I'd play a new role," he replied.

"Doing what?," I asked.

"I'd like to play the part of your first love," he said.

"So you do remember being with me in the World of What Could Be?," I asked.

"Yes, Eve. How would you like to be Jacob the Magician's one and only assistant?, he said.

I was thrilled beyond belief! Naturally, I accepted the offer. Soonafter, we were back stargazing on the hill.

"This is no longer the World of What Could Be, Eve. This is the real world. Our world," said Jacob.

You have got to believe in magic because magic is love.

THE END

ALIEN SCIENCE PROJECT

A Search for World Peace

Chapter 1

Dark with never a sun, Blackforest University was the most reputable college on the aliens' planet. All of the students wore uniforms, as did people on the entire planet. Ann, a science major at the college, was highly intelligent and headstrong. Her favorite teacher, Mr. Lent began this particular day with a new project assignment. He paired the students each with a partner. Ann's partner was Janet who wasn't quite as bright as Ann.

Mr. Lent instructed each group of two to choose a planet to study. It was extremely important not to pick Earth. Mr. Lent made it clear that Earth was forbidden.

"If Earth is studied, you will be ousted from the university. Be forewarned," said Mr. Lent.

Ann was curious about Earth and defied the rules. Janet was a bit of a pushover, so Ann convinced her to choose Earth for their assignment. It didn't take long before Mr. Lent learned of their decision. Janet was spared, but Ann was kicked out from the university that same day. Ann felt that she left unjustifiably.

Several days later, Mr. Lent and his class heard commotion outside. As they approached the windows from the classroom, they witnessed a near riot at the university. Ann led a protest outside with signs that read, "Earth - We want the knowledge". The security guards from the university eventually were able to disband the group.

Prior to that, news reporters filmed Ann and the protesters. A mysterious man saw the news report on television that evening. He was impressed and immediately sent a letter to Ann. The man, Ted, was part of a secret scientific society. The letter stated that he wanted Ann included in the society.

Chapter 2

The planet within the galaxy was never bright, always dark. However, there were lights on the planet, including at the zoo where Ted instructed Ann to meet him. The letter stated that they needed to be inconspicuous so that no one would be suspicious of them. Ted brought bodyguards with him for protection which made Ann a bit nervous. She hoped she was not getting involved in something dangerous, but she was curious to know what the society was all about.

Ted and Ann walked for yards at the zoo. Ted explained that Ann would be trained if she joined the secret society. She was then informed that there would be a flight to Earth.

"When will there be a flight to Earth and why is it off limits?," asked Ann.

She was then interrupted as Ted whispered, "Shh, I think there's a spy. Let's go elsewhere here."

Ted and Ann found a couple of chairs at the zoo where they could further talk. Ted explained that the secret scientific society was still in the experimental stages, but they believed that Earth was better than their dark planet. Suddenly, the zoo lights went dead and shots were heard that were meant for Ted. He quickly grabbed Ann's hand and the two ran out of the premises, along with Ted's body guards.

Chapter 3

People at the zoo were panicking except for Ted. He was cool, calm and collected. Ann assumed he had been through this type of situation before.

Ted, Ann and the body guards ventured to an undisclosed location. Ann did not know where she was. They had traveled through snow to the society's underground headquarters. It was there that Ann witnessed a few hundred scientists performing experiments using technical equipment.

Ted led Ann down a hallway and motioned her to enter a red-colored conference room. A group of about ten people sat around a table as the leader of the meeting spoke. He was a model-type looking man who appeared to be around the same age as Ann. She soon learned that his name was Chase and that he was the head of the entire organization. Once Ann looked in Chase's direction, their eyes immediately connected. Both instantaneously looked away from one another.

Chase began the meeting by introducing Ann to everyone.

"She knows little about this place and what we do," Chase informed the meeting members.

Chase then explained to Ann that he always remains at the society headquarters for his own protection because the secret scientific society was at large. He then assigned Lyn to assist Ann throughout her time at the society headquarters.

As soon as the meeting adjourned, Lyn met with Ann. Lyn stated that the fun part was that she would get to choose a human from Earth to study. She informed Ann that the Earthling would not be aware of this study and that she was to do this for one year. Ann was given the use of a microscopic telescope for research and a microphonic device to hear her human from Earth. Ann chose to study a woman named Angel who had recently graduated from college.

As months rolled by, Ann began to wonder how she exactly got involved in the society and what the purpose was. She eventually approached Chase.

"When will a flight crew be sent to Earth?," asked Ann.

"Soon, Ann. Very soon. First we have to gather all of the data. We are the first to ever do this type of research. You were the last person to be hired here. No one else is allowed through the main doors. Our experiments are still in the beta stage," informed Chase.

Ann wasn't sure her question got answered, but she accepted Chase's reply. Ann continued on with her studies.

Chapter 4

During the course of Ann's studies, she discovered that Earth was only sometimes dark. She was fascinated with the sun, seas, flowers and bees. Although others from the society were assigned to study those things. Ann was to only study Angel.

Ann lived and worked at the society headquarters. Sometimes other people from the planet would lurk outside. Those people were compliant about wearing uniforms; however, inside the society, it was not mandated.

The members of the society were kind to one another. The atmosphere inside was nice, unlike the cold, bitter world outside. Ted was the society's recruiter, Lyn was the tutor, Ann was one of many scientists, and Chase was the head of the entire secret society.

Ann was focused on studying Angel when suddenly Chase announced a flight to Earth the following morning.

"Only seven members can go. Ann, you're one of them," said Chase.

The crew of seven, which included Chase, left the next morning at eleven o'clock. The spaceship traveled beyond lightning speed through galaxies and planets. It only took one day to reach their destination.

Chapter 5

After a safe landing in a deserted area on Earth, the flight crew was greeted. All seven members wore sunglasses as they had been forewarned that their eyes would be sensitive to the sunlight. They had also been advised to be alert of their surroundings at all times. Part of the grand plan stated that Earthlings were not to catch sight of them.

The crew was led to an underground world, once again. There were thousands of people.

"Who are these people and where are we?," Ann asked Chase.

Chase replied, "They are people that are the same as you and I. They are human, just as we are. This is our stake out."

"I don't understand, Chase. We all look the same," said Ann.

"I will explain later," he replied as Chase and Ann stared into the eyes of one another. There was definitely a love interest between the two of them. Chase immediately looked in the other direction and began preparing for the next day.

"Get some sleep for now, Ann. This will be your room. We will resume tomorrow. For now, enjoy the room service," instructed Chase.

Ann was treated just like a queen; however, everything was still a mystery. Eventually, she fell asleep. After waking up and getting ready the following day, Chase instructed Ann to follow her human, Angel, to gain more information. Ann had enough of taking orders.

"I am not about to leave headquarters until I get answers from you, Chase. Why did we travel to Earth through space?," Ann asked.

She was insistent to get answers.

Surprisingly, Chase said, "I'm impressed. Ann, here's the deal. All of us are descendants from Earth. Our ancestors were born here. Long ago on Earth, we were at war with one another. Thus, everyone left and ventured to other planets. They sought world peace by leaving. We now believe in our plan to achieve peace one human at a time. We learned that leaving planet Earth was not the right course of action. The same problems and conflicts developed."

Chapter 6

As previously stated, the plan involved each alien to guide their chosen Earthling towards peace and happiness. Ann was to meet her Earthling face to face. She followed Angel into a park one sunny, summer afternoon. Ann "deviously" approached Angel to ask her about her sports car. The two began a conversation that lasted the remainder of the day. By the time evening approached, Ann and Angel were befriended. They made plans to meet up with one another again; in the meantime, they both went their separate ways.

When Ann returned to headquarters, she was greeted by Chase. He had made dinner for the two of them with one red rose in the center of the table. Ann and Chase stared at one another as they talked into the night. Eventually, Chase gained the courage to ask Ann if she would be his girlfriend.

"In the future, I would be happy to. But for now, I am focusing on my career and my priority of placing peace and happiness into Angel's life," informed Ann.

Just then, the doors flew open. Ann and Chase threw down their coffee cups in shock. The underground world was being attacked. Their location had been traced.

Chapter 7

Ann and Chase had been taken captive. Kevin, the head prison guard, gave no explanation to them or the other six prisoners. In prison, Ann and Chase were mistreated. They were provided with barely enough food and slept on a cold cement floor. At least, Ann and Chase were together. Once in a while they were given outdoor privileges whether it was day or night. The two of them occasionally gazed at the sky together and counted the stars.

"We must develop a plan to escape before it gets worse," Chase said to Ann.

It was during this time that the two of them fell in love. Chase confessed to Ann that he had actually fallen in love with her at first sight. To his surprise, Ann said the same thing back.

Days later in the confines of the prison, Chase was in deep thought. He became adamant that he could not have this prison for Ann. Just as Ann was about to tell Chase her escape plan, Kevin walked in singing as though he hadn't a care in the world. He then gave a stern look and began to drill Chase and Ann for information about their secret organization. Chase refused to say much. Ann stepped in and lied, saying that they, too, were humans from Earth. Chase nodded his head in agreement. Not believing their story, Kevin punched Chase, causing him to fall. This was common behavior. Kevin seemingly liked causing brawls. Though, Chase refused to play his game, remembering that peace, not war, was the aim. Later in the day, Ann informed Chase of her plan to escape nonviolently from prison.

Chapter 8

As several days passed by, the plan was in place. Ann asked one of the prison guards if she could speak to Kevin. The prison guard relayed the message to Kevin who sent back instructions for Ann to meet with him at eleven o'clock. At the meeting, Ann attempted to convince Kevin that Chase and Ann were from Earth and not aliens like the others in the underground world. She informed Kevin that she could prove this based on the fact that she was friends with a human from Earth named Angel. Ann had thrown Kevin a curveball. Kevin wanted more information, so Ann talked about how she met Angel.

Eventually, Kevin ordered his prison workers to find Angel and bring her to the prison. Angel was informed that her friend, Ann, was in custody and thought to be an alien. In an attempt to help her friend, Angel went to the prison to meet with Kevin. She confirmed that Ann was, indeed, her friend and that Chase was a human from Earth as well. Thus, Kevin bent the rules and decided to release Chase and Ann from his captivity.

Chase, Ann and Angel sped fast away in Angel's sports car.

As they passed all of the other cars on the road, Chase said, "I'm impressed, Ann. You found a way to get us out of that place."

Angel dropped Chase and Ann off at a train station. From there, it took a few days before they returned to the secret society. The society members had been greatly concerned for their safety and wellbeing. The society members were relieved to have Chase and Ann back in one piece. As well, Chase and Ann were glad that the others had not been found. All were safe and delighted to be back together.

Chapter 9

Several days after returning to the underground world, Chase informed Ann that there was a mandatory meeting that morning at ten o'clock. The meeting was led by Ken, the head of the entire underworld project.

"Everyone, please be seated. I have an important announcement to make," instructed Ken.

The thousands of society members got situated as Ken continued on.

"Our work on Earth was a mistake. The project is being canceled today. Pack your things and return to your planets. Go to where you came from," he stated.

Everyone had a look of confusion on their face. Chase was furious. His heart began beating at a fast pace as anger erupted within. He nearly knocked Ken to the ground.

"I'm not amused. Why did we work so hard? We will all be laughed at back at our own planets," shouted Chase with tears of anger nearly pouring down his face.

Ken smiled and said, "Thank you, Chase. You just proved my point. Emotions do get the better of people. You see, we have come to a new conclusion. When human beings are born whether on Earth or elsewhere, they possess many different emotions, some good, some bad. The formula to gain peace on Earth is to learn to control these emotions. It appears to be impossible for humans to do so. In fact, we have even witnessed greed within our own society from the gold we have found here. Every place I've traveled is the same. We can't seem to develop world peace. We conclude that it is just an illusion. Our society will now cease."

Ann raised her hand with a question.

"May I say goodbye to Angel before I return to my planet?," she asked.

Ken replied that it would be okay to do so but that it had to be done that same day.

An hour later, Ann entered the radar room in an attempt to locate Angel. Suddenly, the room grew silent with the exception of a loud signal coming from the radar. Members of the society gathered at the radar and whispered to one another. About ten minutes later, Ken turned to the remainder of the members in the room and informed them that a forbidden location had been discovered. Despite the discovery, they were all still instructed to leave.

Chapter 10

The society members all stepped into their spaceships to travel home; however, Chase and Ann never boarded. The two of them were the only aliens left on Earth. They were insistent to find world peace and did not buy into the concepts that coming to Earth was a mistake.

Chase and Ann continued to live in the underground location. Within the radar room, they discovered that Heaven had been the location that was said to be forbidden. Flashing lights and loud sounds from the radar continued to point to Heaven. Though they were not convinced that they would be doomed if they were to visit. Chase and Ann looked at one another with excitement.

"Do you realize what has been discovered with this equipment?," asked Chase to Ann.

"Yes, we have found Heaven," she replied.

"Do you think that if we just visited Heaven for a day it would be okay?," Chase asked.

"Yes, but it's not going to be of any value as we create our plan for peace," Ann said.

The two of them put the subject to rest for a while as they began to develop their plan. They brainstormed about how the world could be stable. Chase and Ann thought for hours, but peace seemed to be out of their control. They could not figure out a way for peace and happiness everyday. Chase and Ann almost gave up hope too. They were beginning to find coping to be difficult. It was a shot in the dark, but they concluded that their last chance was to visit Heaven.

The following day, Chase and Ann followed the radar which led to Heaven's gates. As they reached for the handle, they entered into a nightmare. The gate was locked. Just then, Chase told Ann to have no fear. He had a plan.

Chase used his pocket knife and jimmied open the Gates of Heaven. Ann and Chase slightly hesitated, then slowly entered the inside to Heaven. It was endlessly big and wide.

"Amazing!," said Chase and Ann together as they glared.

The two were in awe.

CHAPTER 11

The visions and sounds in Heaven were profound. Just ahead, Ann saw Angel and a Man in the distance. Angel approached Chase and Ann and informed them that the Man was God. As they drew closer to Him, He appeared to have a smile. Chase was so nervous he could barely walk.

Ann decided to talk to God.

"Pardon me, Sir. Do you have a few spare moments?," she asked.

God paused briefly from his task of listening to prayers. Ann then took the opportunity to confess to God her sins. She told Him that she had lied in order to escape prison.

God said, "And don't forget you pried your way into Heaven as well," as He brightly smiled. "Ann, you are delivered. And what did you want to speak to me about?"

"World peace," said Ann.

"Granted," God firmly said without hesitation.

God then told his two children, Chase and Ann, to take a bow for being so brave. He said, though, that they must leave Heaven and return home.

Chase and Ann left with smiles. God definitely had a unique style. Chase and Ann flew back to their planet. World peace was in existence there. People on their planet applauded them and hailed Chase and Ann as heroes. All of a sudden, a star shined which brightly lit up their planet. Everyone was happy and content.

Each planet in every galaxy was at peace. All wars had ceased. Eternal serenity was everywhere. White flags waved, flowers bloomed and calm waters moved the oceans.

THE END

I TRAVELED FAR WITHIN A BOOK

A Story of Self Love

Chapter 1

As I finished reading one page of a book that I had been assigned to read, it spent the remainder of the days and weeks on my nightstand. I found the book to be dull and bleak. Thus, my teacher was outraged that I had not completed the assignment.

"Read a book by tomorrow!," instructed my teacher.

I dreaded reading as I found it to be boring. Reluctant to go, I walked to the local community library to borrow a book. My legs were stampeding as I entered the door. To my surprise, lights flashed on and off as confetti poured down on me. Even a small marching band greeted me with a key. I turned towards the librarian and read her name tag which said, "Marian." I then spoke to her.

"What is the purpose for the key?," I asked.

"Later you will see," Marian responded.

As I stepped further into the library, the band became silent. I glanced at people standing in rows throughout the entire library. My curiosity arose. As I approached Marian to ask her if I had entered the wrong place, I hesitated. She became busy entering books into a database. I decided not to disturb her and, instead, I wandered around the library. *I was astounded and wondered to myself why I was surrounded with people all in rows.* It occurred to me that each person was standing where a book should be. My curiosity continued to expand.

Chapter 2

The sign read, "Nonfiction 7.00" as I moved slowly near an aisle of books. I noticed that this particular aisle accommodated rows lined mostly with men. As I approached one man, I then stood directly in front of him. I decided to begin a conversation. I asked him about his baseball cap; however, he ignored the question and instructed me to choose a page number. I picked page thirty four and suddenly, the man began to rap. He recited World Series game statistics and stated the name of the author. The man ended by saying, "with peace and brotherly love." I responded by thanking him before glancing further at my surroundings.

I became increasingly confident that the people in rows were actual books to talk to for free. I decided to test the same man's knowledge of a different subject.

"Can you please give me facts about domestic violence?," I asked.

The man stood in silence. Thus, I wandered over to a different section of the library where I would choose a book for my assignment. I stood in front of people in a row labeled, "Biographies". They all looked interesting as I wondered which one to choose. Several minutes passed by before I decided on the biography of a famous legend. Just then, I heard a whisper coming from the row labeled, "Geography". A woman lined in a row confessed to me that she had a secret crush on a man in Row Three which was on the other side of the aisle.

As a librarian walked past, the woman began reciting facts about oceans and lakes. After the librarian was gone from view, the woman continued on about her crush. I interrupted her to speak.

"Who is your secret crush?," I asked.

She replied, "I seek knowledge of a man from books about relationships. I had once been returned to the wrong section, right next to him. Our eyes instantly connected and we talked to one another for hours. Please keep quiet about this though."

"Why are you telling me all of this?," I further asked.

As the woman cried oceans, she said, "I want to become his girlfriend, but I need some help. He has an array of knowledge about relationships as though he has a college degree. Again, keep your lips zipped about this, please."

I promised the woman that I would find a way for the two of them to later date. In the meantime, I felt compelled to talk to a book from Row Eight.

Chapter 3

It was in Row Eight that I found books on poetry. This library adventure was a great opportunity to talk to a vast number of books. I realized that each book only knew what was inside of them - a bit of knowledge.

I talked to different books for hours on various subjects. I had vast interest in each one. Later, I discovered the power of knowledge.

It was time to make my selections. After choosing my books, I walked over to the check-out counter. Quietly, I spoke to the librarian, stating that I thoroughly enjoyed my encounter at the library. Suddenly, I remembered that I had made a promise to a book in the Geography section. While Marian was busy typing up my membership card, I stepped into the section and took the book. I then walked to the opposite side of the aisle to take the book of the woman's secret crush.

The book whispered, "Thank you very much."

Upon my return to the check-out counter, Marian handed me my membership card. My books were standing closely by my side as though they were guards. I had only one question for Marian before leaving the library.

"What is your question?," asked Marian.

"What about the key?," I asked.

Marian stated that the key had been given to me because it was the key to the Book of Me. What an amazing library experience this had been. I was excited to show my classmates my newest friends of books and flaunt the knowledge I was gaining. I was forever hooked on books from that day forward.

Chapter 4

Mist rose from the floor and people in rows returned to being paper books at the moment I walked out of the library. I turned back to take a second look. Sure enough, as I peered into the library window, all of the books were made of paper. Snow began to lightly fall.

Upon my return home, I entered the den while the geography and relationship books went on their first date. In the meantime, I read my poetry book.

I realized what the library had been teaching me. The lesson was that I had simply been missing the key to who I was and my entire being. Thereafter, I searched my soul and found joy and laughter. I stole my own heart as I traveled far within a book.

THE END

BROKEN DREAMS AND MAGIC SCHEMES

A Magical Love Story

Chapter 1

Here is the story's setting and scene. Inside a small apartment located in Minnesota, a woman in her forties sat staring out her window. The woman, Dakota, was depressed and not too lean. She had been crying on and off for four years. The reason for her tears was that boyfriend, Maxwell, ended their relationship. Dakota appeared to be emotionally put together to others; however, within herself she felt ruined.

Having a case of depression, Dakota spent little time on housekeeping. Her daily routine began by waking up, eating breakfast, and praying. She spent the remainder of the day reminiscing of the times she shared with Maxwell. Her heart had been deeply broken.

Dakota's daughter, Paige, was twenty-two years old. She lived on her own, leaving Dakota to herself. Paige had been born shortly after Dakota married Rob. They later divorced. Soon after, she fell in love with her heartthrob, Maxwell.

Chapter 2

Here is the story's beginning. As bright lights lit up the New York City skyline, Dakota's career was reaching new heights. She was twenty-four years of age and not yet a mother.

Dakota was a top-notch financial consultant at one of the world's most well-known fashion design companies, Remy Harrington Designs. Maxwell had hired her over dinner and wine. He was an arrogant, high-level executive and drove a sports car with a thundering, first-class sound system. Maxwell had the best of everything. He was the most sought after bachelor in Manhattan. Dakota found him fascinating; more so than her boyfriend, Rob.

Rob was a personal fitness trainer which did not fit the ideal career that Dakota wished for the man she was dating. She was extremely materialistic; however, she also exuded a trait for being realistic.

After work each night, Dakota met up with her best friend, Stan. He performed magic and comedy at Ray's Bar and Grill where Dakota got together with him. Stan was a bit nerdy, yet he was a loyal friend and always kept his promises. Dakota maintained his friendship because she could always rely on him.

Stan was disabled, having only his left arm. He was, indeed, the nicest man Dakota ever knew. Anytime she needed a friend to talk to, Stan was there for her. Rob, her boyfriend, never showed jealousy, as he was preoccupied with work at the fitness center. Part of his job involved training professional athletes. Though his true character would later surface.

Chapter 3

Rob and Dakota married after she announced her pregnancy. Dakota was thrilled to be a mother ever since Paige entered the world. On the other hand, it saddened her to know that she had lost any potential opportunity to ever date Maxwell.

Stan got little applause each night after performing magic tricks and telling jokes. He was a bit geeky, unlike Maxwell the hotshot. After Paige was born, Dakota and Stan grew apart. Rob had become controlling and commanded Dakota to break away from Stan, stating that she should not be friends with a man. Dakota felt smothered.

Eventually, Dakota asserted herself and filed for divorce. Thus, her marriage ended and Stan and Dakota rekindled their friendship. Dakota was happy on her own as a single mother. Throughout all the events in her life, she continued to work for Maxwell in New York City. She had hired a nanny to take care of Paige during the days she worked. Annie was the name of her nanny.

Stan showed up at Dakota's high-rise Manhattan apartment one day to simply talk. Suddenly, Annie pulled up a chair to join the conversation. She did this routinely when Stan visited. Annie's flirtatious gestures were noticeable. It was obvious that Annie liked Stan to no measure. For a split second, Dakota felt a bit of jealousy. Immediately, she turned away as though she was blind and blocked it out of her mind.

"Stan is only a friend," Dakota repeated within her head.

Chapter 4

Dakota's life was on an upward spiral that nearly hit rock bottom the day that Maxwell stormed into her office. He was stern and told Dakota to meet him at eight o'clock that night. Dakota was nervous, but she felt she had no choice since Maxwell was her boss.

Dakota and Maxwell met for dinner at a ritzy Manhattan restaurant. Maxwell was being arrogant as always. For some reason, Dakota was attracted to his behavior. Maxwell began the meeting by ordering scotch for himself. He then informed Dakota that the company financial reports were in and that sales were declining steadily.

"Dakota, you're the only one, no doubt, who can pull Remy Harrington Designs out of this mess," stated Maxwell.

Dakota had the perfect clout to hire a new financial team. Not much time had passed since they sat down to dinner yet, Maxwell was already ordering a second scotch.

"The company is in your hands, Dakota. Don't mess this up or else you'll be milking cows back in your hometown in Minnesota," he said.

Dakota ordered her first glass of wine. After an hour of chatting with Maxwell over dinner, Dakota had a brilliant idea for resolving the financial crisis. Maxwell was so impressed by her plan, as well as her beauty, that he asked Dakota to be his girlfriend. She readily accepted. Dakota's dreams were complete. She had a lucrative career, a high-rise Manhattan apartment and a wonderful daughter. Additionally, she had captured the most desired eligible bachelor in New York City.

Dakota's life could not be brighter. She was definitely a go-getter, working overtime into the night to fix the financial crisis. She displayed determination and perseverance.

One evening, Dakota was interrupted by a phone call from Stan. He talked about his performance that night at the bar. Stan claimed he had been fired due to adding singing to his routine. Dakota showed compassion and support for Stan. The two met that night and talked into the morning hours. Stan was ever so grateful for their friendship.

"That's what friends are for. They spend time with you when you're down," said Dakota.

Stan had always been enthralled with Dakota. However, it was Maxwell who had her heart. That morning, Dakota was late to work and wore the same clothes as the prior day. She missed a mandatory meeting. Dakota apologized to Maxwell.

"I'm sorry. I lost track of time," she stated.

Maxwell was outraged. He believed she was lying and that she had been out all night cheating on him. Maxwell broke up with Dakota as well as firing her. He told her he would ruin her name within the industry. Thus, it was nearly impossible for Dakota to be hired anywhere else in New York City.

Dakota's heart broke into a million pieces. After taking care of Paige, she barely had strength left to take care of herself. Dakota and Paige boarded a train in the pouring rain and headed to Minnesota.

Chapter 5

After Maxwell had broken up with Dakota, she developed deep depression. She sat at home each day, staring out the window with a broken heart. Dakota began to grow bitter. She thought all men were the same and that women were merely a game to them. Dakota adjusted to a different lifestyle in Minnesota. On a daily basis, she talked to no one except for Stan. He called everyday to check up on her. Stan had never fallen for Annie. It had been Dakota whom he always loved. Stan thought that to win her love, he had to be clever.

One morning, specifically at ten o'clock, Dakota's phone rang. It was Stan on the other end.

"Look outside your window. You're not alone," Stan instructed.

Dakota looked outside as her smile grew bigger and brighter. Stan was serenading her on the lawn like the perfect gentleman. Dakota greeted Stan with a hug. Stan then rolled out a red carpet.

"What is this for?," asked Dakota.

"You said that you no longer believe in love. Dakota, I am here to prove you wrong and show you that love still exists. Take my hand, my friend. I will guide you into a world of magic," replied Stan.

Thus, down the red carpet Stan and Dakota walked. Up ahead appeared a glittering door. Dakota was no longer depressed. As Stan continued holding her hand, he led Dakota to a place with a band.

"Where are we? Have we left Minnesota?," asked Dakota.

"We are in a magical fantasy library where there are rooms with shelves filled with stories and poetry. It is here that I will prove that love still exists," said Stan.

Chapter 6

Stan and Dakota walked down a hallway and into a red-colored conference room. They were not greeted by the meeting members after entering the room. Stan and Dakota were invisible to them. Stan and Dakota then witnessed two people, Ann and Chase, falling in love at first sight.

Dakota asked, "Are we in a fable?"

Stan replied, "We are in the story 'Alien Science Project' within this library."

Dakota was highly impressed, although Stan suggested that they leave the conference room and return outside to walk further down the red carpet. This time, they entered into a poem within the magical fantasy library. Dakota was having the time of her life. She questioned to herself if she should keep Stan as only a friend. At that moment, she decided to give Stan a kiss.

"This adventure is so much fun!," exclaimed Dakota as she ran further down the red carpet and into another poem.

CHAPTER 7

Stan and Dakota held hands as they ventured in and out of various stories. Stan had won the heart of Dakota.

"You're a charming man. I'm in love with you, Stan," said Dakota.

Stan's heart was fluttering. He then handed a priceless piece of jewelry to Dakota. It was an engagement ring that had once belonged to his grandmother.

Dakota answered, "Yes," after Stan asked her to marry him.

Though, Dakota thought this was not reality.

"This is a world of fantasy. Will we still be engaged after returning to Minnesota and back into reality?," asked Dakota.

"Allow me to clear up your confusion. Reality is also here. You see, no matter where you are, you can look up at the stars. Not everything inside the magical fantasy library is happy. There are sad stories and poems as well.

The time to return to Minnesota had drawn near. Stan and Dakota walked back on the red carpet. Although Stan informed Dakota there was enough time to venture into one more story. Dakota chose, "The Ride of Our Lives," where she met Abigail, Nicole, Grace and Jane.

Stan and Dakota attended the county fair within the story. They only stayed a few minutes as the magic spell was nearly over.

"We must return to Minnesota immediately," Stan said.

Dakota and Stan entered the glittering door which was plain on the other side. Stan then rolled up the red carpet.

"The magical fantasy library was fun," said Dakota.

Stan added, "Magic is here everyday too."

"Stan, I love you," said Dakota.

"I love you too, but it is time for me to return home for now," he said.

Chapter 8

Dakota began planning her wedding. In the meantime, Stan had returned to New York City. Dakota called him so that they could plan their honeymoon.

"Where would you like to go?," asked Stan.

"To the library again," replied Dakota.

"A honeymoon at a library?," Stan asked with laughter.

Dakota replied, "Yes."

Soon after, Dakota began to focus on her health and weight loss. She had finally recovered from her broken heart and she was ready to straighten out her life.

Months rolled by as Dakota continued to lose weight. She began to get glares from men everywhere she went. For fun, Dakota and Paige shopped together. To survive, Dakota eventually opened her own clothing store. She wondered to herself why she had wasted so many years crying for Maxwell. Dakota began to look at love a different way. It was as though she was seeing Stan for the first time. She realized he was quite handsome with great talent. She began to regret the fact that she had not realized this sooner.

Chapter 9

Stan and Dakota agreed to a honeymoon at the library. Stan used his magic and was able to make a deal with the author of this story. The author was to write a poem about a location which Stan and Dakota could use as the place for their honeymoon. The agreement was that Stan would return a favor. He would make sure to use his magic to give the author a winning lottery ticket.

The author wrote a poem about a hotel overlooking the ocean. The sound of congas and bongos played as the warm breeze moved the leaves of the palm trees. The poem created the ideal place for a honeymoon.

Stan and Dakota were married in the month of June. The wedding was elegant, romantic, and brought tears of joy. The vows were deeply meaningful. Dakota was proud to have Paige as her Maid of Honor.

After the wedding, Stan and Dakota ventured to the library and vacationed for free. They entered into a poem entitled, "Honeymoon Getaway", which the author had written just for them. They spent ten days there; however, time moves fast. Ten days had passed by and the honeymoon was over. However, Stan had one more surprise for Dakota. They drove to a lovely new home in Minnesota.

As Dakota walked through the door, she saw nothing in the house except a lottery ticket on the floor. Stan owned up to his end of the bargain. He had used sleight of hand to give the author of this story a winning ticket!

THE END

HEART FOR HIRE

The Story of an Independent Woman

CHAPTER 1

The Advertisement

The sign by the gate leading to the mansion read, "Butler, Doorman, Limo Driver, Maid, Maintenance Man, Personal Financial Adviser, Chef, Personal Fitness Trainer, Gardener, Pilot and Heart for Hire."

Miss Independent, Caroline, was in search of new employees. She had been nicknamed "Miss Independent" because she was a self-assured woman and carried herself with confidence. Though Miss Independent depended on each one of her employees. She formed a strong bond with some of them yet, everyone of them ended up leaving.

I told Caroline every time I saw her that she's got to believe. Who am I you wonder? I was Caroline's personal therapy counselor. I have spent countless sessions with her. Never do I share confidential information as I have taken an oath; however, Caroline has allowed me to tell her story in hopes of helping someone else.

Miss Independent was diagnosed as co-dependent. Needless to say, she is a wealthy woman. She inherited her riches at the tender age of fifteen after the death of her grandfather. Since then, Caroline has never held a job longer than a month. She rarely lifts a finger and finds ways to get others to do everything for her.

Caroline is the envy of her town. No one knows the truth that her life is sad and lonely. She lives by herself in a mansion which lies on several acres of land. She is a bit eccentric as she has builders add expansions whenever she gets bored.

Allow me to explain the reason why Caroline has been advertising for help. Her story is enlightening and inspiring.

CHAPTER 2

The Pilot

Caroline owns a private jet with no one to fly it. Years ago, she was married to a pilot. They often traveled to other states and other countries for vacation. One fatal day while up in the air, without warning, her husband shouted.

"Caroline - steer," ordered her husband.

He was experiencing severe health issues and became unable to fly the jet. Caroline had never flown a jet before. Her husband, while clutching his heart, gave her instructions.

"One direction," he said.

Though Caroline kept flying in circles. Eventually, with his guidance, the jet safely landed. Her husband was rushed to the hospital where he later died.

Caroline suffers from Post-Traumatic Stress Disorder and high anxiety as a result of her experience. She talked about the loss of her husband quite a bit. I asked her what she would say to him if she had the chance. She responded by saying that she would tell him, "I need someone like you." From there, Caroline went on to say that he made loving easy. She feared that she would never know how to love again.

Chapter 3

The Butler and The Maid

The Butler and the Maid were no longer employed at Caroline's mansion. Although, they both left on good terms with bonus pay. Caroline had played "the matchmaker" and encouraged the two to date. It backfired on her though.

To her surprise, the Butler and Maid announced, "I quit."

They had made a successful love connection. Their plan was to get married and move out of state.

Caroline was invited to the wedding which was the last time she saw them before saying "Goodbye." This is why a Butler and Maid were on the list for hire.

Chapter 4

The Chef

Caroline's mansion became quieter once the Chef left for good. He was an overly social man who kept the place alive. Caroline was so desperate for him to return back to working for her that she even studied online to learn magic. Because of the stress she endured, her thinking became unclear. She thought that by learning magic she could somehow bring the Chef back.

The Chef was an older gentleman and decided to retire, leaving Caroline to cook for one. She bought a cookbook, but burned most everything she tried to make. Sometimes she went without meals to avoid cooking. Caroline longed for a hero.

Chapter 5

The Doorman

The Doorman no longer worked for Caroline. Let me explain the situation that occurred.

The Doorman was known to be a ladies' man. He dated countless women and sometimes entered into more than one relationship at a time. Caroline felt she would never date again; however, two years after her husband died, the Doorman asked her out for dinner. Their date led to a short relationship.

The Doorman spent most of his work day chatting with other women on his phone. Since Caroline did not receive many visitors, the Doorman had plenty of time on his hands to socialize. Caroline was faithful throughout the relationship, but the Doorman cheated.

Caroline became suspicious, so she set a trap which the Doorman fell into. She caught him cheating. What made matters worse was that he lied about it. Thus, Caroline ended the relationship and fired him.

CHAPTER 6

The Gardener

The gardens at Caroline's mansion were mostly empty. She addressed the issue with the Gardener who was usually out in left field. He planted flower seeds and spent his work days talking to them instead of watering them.

He told Caroline, "A little love is all they need."

Yet, nothing would grow. Caroline suspected that the Gardener had a drinking problem.

He howled at the gardens saying, "Let it shine," as he held a bottle of booze.

Eventually, he left the job and entered a program for alcoholics. To this day, Caroline continues to pay his way. She felt obligated to do so being his employer as well as having concern for his well being. Thus, she was in search of a new Gardener.

CHAPTER 7

The Limo Driver

Caroline was a fast-paced woman. When she had somewhere to go, she wanted to spend little time on travel. Her Limo Driver drove too slow which filled Caroline with frustration. She kept her emotions well hidden, though she wished he would drive faster. Therefore, her plans for the job interviews were to make certain the people were fast drivers.

In addition to the Limo Driver's slow pace, he was headstrong and did things his own way, disregarding her orders. She later realized he had passive-aggressive behavior. When the limo broke down for good, Caroline gave the Limo Driver the responsibility to make the deal on a new limo. She knew nothing about cars or mechanics.

Instead of a limo, the driver returned to the mansion with a car that had previously been used as a taxi. After enforcing to him that she sought for a limo, he returned the taxi to the dealership and brought back a bus.

Caroline had speculated that the Limo Driver was jealous of her wealth and therefore, he did these things on purpose. Caroline is loyal to the people in her life; however, she fired him and purchased a white limo herself.

Chapter 8

The Maintenance Man

The Maintenance Man approached Caroline to tell her he was quitting. Prior to leaving, he confided in Caroline that his lover had left him to move to Texas.

He said, "She's gone. It's a heartache."

The Maintenance Man and Caroline were best friends. She tried to console him through his loss. Since Caroline had taken lessons in magic, she played her magic flute in hopes that his lover would return. The Maintenance Man found humor in her attempt, but Caroline was serious about it.

As luck would have it, the Maintenance Man's lover returned to him. He thanked Caroline endlessly.

"I appreciate your efforts. I was at the point of nearly giving up and becoming a monk," he said.

The Maintenance Man said that his lover returned for him so that he would join her in Texas where her family lived. Thus, he left the maintenance job to move along with his lover.

Caroline was left to do repair work herself. Being a high-maintenance woman, she stopped to get her nails done before venturing to the library. She borrowed two books called, "Service and Repair" and "How to Fight Loneliness."

Chapter 9

Personal Financial Adviser

Caroline's Personal Financial Adviser also left town. In his youth, the adviser lived in poverty. Therefore, he was compelled to become a millionaire in his adult life. The Personal Financial Adviser was sly and greedy. He played upon Caroline's good heart. He would continually tell her about his own money issues. She felt sympathetic and gave him money to help his situation every time.

The Personal Financial Adviser was flirtatious with Caroline. He complimented her on her beauty and intelligence. Caroline felt special but displayed modesty. She developed a love interest in him. They never entered into a relationship with one another as Caroline discovered he was a married man. The Personal Financial Adviser had been hiding the fact that he was married. He would even take off his wedding ring before his meetings with Caroline.

After robbing his clients of their money, the Personal Financial Adviser did, indeed, become a millionaire. In an effort to never be caught, he moved to Florida. Caroline was left to manage her money on her own.

Chapter 10

Personal Fitness Trainer

Caroline and her Personal Fitness Trainer shared each other's hearts until the day he shamed her in front of a crowd. This occurred the first time they ever went dancing together.

Having full awareness that she lacked talent for dancing, Caroline felt self conscious. *She thought to herself, "Maybe I can focus my mind and energies into a magical trance and, with enough concentration, have the ability to dance."*

Caroline insisted her magic was real and danced like never before. The crowd singled her out on the dance floor and began calling Miss Independent by a different nickname. They called her the Dancing Queen.

Caroline did not know her Personal Fitness Trainer well enough to realize he was a narcissist. He had the need to outshine her. When the attention was all on Caroline, the Personal Fitness Trainer felt jealous and intimidated. As a result, he purposely nudged her while the spotlight was on her, causing her to fall. He was condescending and laughed as she fumbled while standing back up.

Those events were only the first glimpse she got of his true character. Though, it was just enough for her to end their romantic and working relationships. Caroline had since gained some weight. Thus, she became in search of a new Personal Fitness Trainer.

Chapter 11

Caroline

Caroline was left to temporarily take over every job role herself. For the first time in her life, she truly did become independent.

Caroline actually took the time to open the cookbook and teach herself how to cook healthy meals. She spent all of her time occupying three rooms in the mansion; therefore, she only had to clean and maintain those three rooms. She learned money management and watered the gardens. Instead of riding in a limo, she drove herself to the store.

Caroline got back in shape by walking around the perimeters of her home everyday. The only role she didn't play was that of a pilot. She still has occasional flashbacks of her traumatic flying experience and; therefore, she has no desire to obtain a pilot license.

One by one, she crossed out each occupation from her advertisement. Eventually, the sign read, "Pilot and Heart for Hire."

I don't meet with Caroline anymore. I miss her and feel sadness for myself. Most of my clients never leave counseling. Caroline overcame obstacles through her determined attitude. I wish I could take the credit for the strong, independent woman she blossomed into, but I only played a part. Caroline exceeded all expectations and she was no longer in need of my help. Instead, she became her own hero.

I drove by her mansion the other day. The sign is still outside by the gate. I am certain Caroline will soon find a new pilot whom she can love and never again need to advertise "Heart for Hire."

THE END

A HOLIDAY TRILOGY

A Valentine's Day Story

Chapter 1

Feeling down and lonely, I turned to my favorite Cincinnati radio station. Each consecutive song being played was sad on the day to celebrate love. It was Valentine's Day 2017.

As I was about to switch the station, the DJ announced, "Here I am."

Previously from New York City, Jenny was the new kid on the block. Her first night shift broadcast at WMME, Magic Mix Entertainment Radio, had begun. Suddenly, upbeat music was being played. They were songs I was unaware of. The sound was different than anything I had ever heard before.

Jenny's voice was welcoming.

She said on air, "Call me with song requests."

Chapter 2

Jenny became frustrated when every requested song was sad.

She shouted, "Listen everyone! Stop requesting sad songs. It's Valentine's Day for God's sake."

Yet, people continued to ask for sad songs to be played. Finally, Jenny had enough.

She said, "Hold on. Let me tell you about love."

The people of Cincinnati began turning up the volume on their radios. They were curious about what Jenny had to say.

"I have a midnight confession. This is my true story. My life was down in flames. I played with fire by befriending the devil. It began when I visited a gypsy woman to have my fortune read. I sat down at a table with her face to face. The gypsy glared intensely into a crystal ball.

A voice whispered, 'She talks to angels.'

The gypsy raised her head to address me. She said I give love a bad name.

I sought life's answers from psychics, gypsies, tarot card readers, just to name a few. I believed them to possess great power. I never got the answers I desired and life went from bad to worse every time.

My story has a twist. After hitting rock bottom, I took a shot in the dark and wrote a letter to God out of desperation. I wrote, 'Dear God. Send me an angel.' I then heard a voice say, 'It's in God's hands.' Music that only I could hear began playing," Jenny said on air.

Jenny continued to broadcast her letter to God.

She said, "I then wrote, 'Please give Cupid one more arrow to be used on me.' I signed the letter, 'Girl on Fire' and then added, 'P.S. I love you'".

Chapter 3

After Jenny had completed telling about the letter, she broadcast about the note she had written.

She said, "I wrote, 'Dear Life. Does it get better?' A voice replied to me, 'God only knows'. I signed the note, 'A Piece of Work'. Suddenly, I heard 'Boom Boom' and saw the crash of lightning. Voices loomed overhead saying, 'Hear us from Heaven. You possess a voice within. Your guardian angel is there – your angel without wings.'"

The night shift continued. Jenny took a break from broadcasting her story to play a few songs on air. She dedicated the songs to her angel without wings – her guardian angel within. Jenny resumed her broadcast.

She said, "I heard the ringing of one bell. I was certain it meant my angel got its wings."

Jenny played two more love songs. The audience remained listening throughout the night. Her shift was nearing its end. She played one more song called, "My Secret Valentine". When the song was over, she realized she had enough time left to take a few calls from her listeners.

"Call me," she said on air.

Just then, Jenny received an off air call from God. She nearly fell to her knees. He requested the song, "I Am Your Friend."

Chapter 4

Jenny continued to play music on air into the early morning hours. She was working overtime. The songs were about hope, inspiration and love. The audience listened intensely. No one switched stations.

Jenny broadcasted saying, "Everyday is yours to win."

It gave the people of Cincinnati belief in love once more. As the broadcast cut to commercial, an old, grouchy man called into the station.

"Shut up!," he shouted into the phone.

The man was incredibly rude and even addressed Jenny by the wrong name.

"Sam, play music and stop broadcasting as if I am ignorant and in need of your education. This isn't a talk show," said the old man.

I had been listening to Jenny's entire broadcast and also called in to request a few songs during commercial break. Jenny seemed as though a friend even though we had never met. She then played a song about magic.

Jenny's shift was done. She thought she had failed. While walking into the morning sun, she hailed a taxi. Jenny was bound for New York City. She felt unappreciated from sharing her story on air.

A big part of Jenny's life was music. Inside the taxi, she asked the driver to turn up the radio. Sweet songs played when suddenly the sound of breaking news interrupted the broadcast.

The reporter said, "Who was she? She's gone."

During the weeks to follow, the song requests were not all sad. Ever since Jenny's broadcast, the people of Cincinnati began falling in love. She had turned the whole city around without ever knowing the impact she made.

A THANKSGIVING STORY: THE PRAYER

Chapter 1

Jenny lived in New York City and was usually sad and lonely. Her long-distance relationship with Tyler had lasted three years thus far. Instead of making Jenny feel special, he rarely made time for her. Jenny was so in love; however, Tyler never verbally agreed to a committed relationship. Jenny wanted clarification, so she mustered up the courage to ask Tyler if he considered their relationship to be serious. During the course of their phone conversation, Tyler avoided ever answering her question.

Jenny had previously driven hundreds of miles to visit Tyler on three separate occasions. Tyler, on the other hand, never stepped foot in New York City. Jenny's friends gave her emotional support as she cried pouring tears about her love life. Her friends suggested that she spend less time dwelling and start having some fun. They brought her to an amusement park.

Jenny was afraid of heights, so her friends coaxed her to ride the roller coaster. They assured her it would be safe. On the way up on the ride, Jenny prayed to God. Suddenly, Jenny fell! People screamed at the sight of Jenny lying nearly lifeless on the ground. Her tragedy made top national news. After Tyler heard about the incident, his heart rate increased rapidly. He drove hundreds of miles to New York for the first time.

Tyler shouted, "Doctor, doctor, have you seen Jenny?," after rushing to the hospital.

Tyler found Jenny's room and held her hand. She didn't speak a word as she laid in a coma. Her chances for survival were questionable. The doctors thought that if she did survive, she would probably never walk again.

"Babe, I'm depending on you. Open those beautiful eyes of blue," said Tyler.

Tyler sat by Jenny's bedside for hours. Suddenly, her heart monitor flat lined.

"Someone get me a doctor!," shouted Tyler.

Doctors and nurses rushed into her room; though there was no sign of life. *Tyler thought to himself, "How could I have let her down?"* Dr. Wu told Tyler to wait in the waiting room. The doctor later informed him that Jenny had been revived but would probably be in a coma forever. Tyler became frantic.

"Dr. Wu, you need to realize her life is a song. Have you ever been in love? Send in the clowns, the entertainers, radios, a guitar player, a piano man," Tyler frantically insisted.

Dr. Wu replied, "Mister, Mister, you must leave. Stop causing a stir."

CHAPTER 2

Tyler left the hospital, but instead of traveling home, he took a flight to Rome. Upon entering a Roman church, he prayed out loud for a miracle – one that could melt icicles. Priest Danny overheard his prayer. Tyler told the priest about Jenny, his girlfriend.

"Angel of Mercy. Don't give up on us yet," said Tyler as he continued to pray.

Holy man Danny addressed Tyler and said, "God is a DJ. What are your favorite songs?"

Tyler replied, "Songs she never heard of – 'A Magical Dream' and 'Because You Live.'"

Chapter 3

While Tyler spent time in Rome, a celebration broke out at the hospital. Jenny had come back to life. She was no longer in a coma. It was a Thanksgiving Day miracle.

Jenny continued to improve during the following days and weeks. Her goal was to be home for Christmas. In the name of love, Jenny had been blessed by God.

A CHRISTMAS STORY: BABY, PLEASE COME HOME

Chapter 1

As the December sun rose in Rome, Tyler lit candles to pray. Upon learning of Jenny's recovery, he rushed back to the United States. At the time he landed, Tyler called Jenny at the hospital as snow began to fall.

"Baby, come home. I'm lost without you. Let's stay together," said Tyler.

Rapidly, the weather turned into a snow storm. Tyler and Jenny's phone call was disconnected. In desperation to see Jenny, Tyler rented a car. He was determined to drive through snow just to be at her side. Tyler struggled to stay warm after the car heater broke. The snow fell faster and faster. He continued to try calling Jenny, but the phone was out of service. The car eventually got stuck in a snow drift.

Tyler prayed to God and then walked through snow in the bitter cold. The temperature was ten below. He was weary and fell into a snowbank. He repeated the words, "Hold on" as he drifted away into a deep sleep. Inside his head, Tyler heard spirit voices and saw the vision of an angel. For a brief moment, Tyler left this world. While in the afterlife, he made a pact to himself to change.

He said to God, "If you let me live, I will give Jenny eternal love."

Chapter 2

Three weeks had passed. Jenny's wish came true. She was back home right before Christmas. Although, Tyler was not there with her. Once again in her life, she hadn't heard from him. She assumed he had changed his mind about her.

Jenny tried to hide the heartache she felt. Suddenly, the doorbell rang. Christmas carolers softly, yet beautifully, sang. Standing in the back of the group - there he was! Tyler was dressed in a suit and tie. The carolers paused in silence as bells rang.

Tyler took Jenny's hand. He was never going to let her go. Often, it takes misfortune and heartache to wake up and see the light. God's love had been with them all along brighter than the sun.

THE END

CLASS ACT

An Educational Story

Chapter 1

Home Room

Buzz was the sound I heard coming from my alarm clock. It was another day for high school. My bedroom was surrounded with papers from my writing and rewriting an essay. I could not miss the bus as this was an important day. I was to read my essay out loud to the class.

An hour later, I arrived at school. I had prayed to my Creator that I had not forgotten to bring my essay. I ran down the hall in an effort to not be late to the Home Room. If I was not punctual, the school staff would write me up and hand me a warning. Luckily, I made it to my desk in time.

Some of my classmates spent the time in the Home Room brushing their hair and chatting with one another. My Home Room teacher, Miss Woods, wrote a daily quote which she read to the class. "Make each day count" was the quote of that particular day. Those were the only words that Miss Woods spoke. I believe she never said much so that her short words sunk into our heads.

Later, I searched my backpack and found my essay. As I began browsing the paper, the bell rang. Home Room was over and I was onto my next class. I wasn't a shy person. Instead, I had the confidence to sing as I walked down the hallway.

CHAPTER 2

Psychology

I made it to my class on time. The Psychology teacher, Mr. Byron, taught about the brain. He stated that he enjoyed teaching; however, I found learning to be a pain.

Mr. Byron began his lesson by saying, "There are five things you must know about your mind. They are (1) Our brains do not know the difference between reality and imagination. It reacts to whatever you think about."

I turned to the classmate sitting across from me and joked that I should go to mental therapeutic rehabilitation and get out of this class.

Mr. Byron went on to say (2) You experience what your mind consumes the most time thinking. Therefore, think positive thoughts. Your brain pattern will change and adjust to your new way to thinking. (3) Your brain runs mostly on autopilot. Negative thoughts create anxiety and stress. Let me restate to think positively often. (4) It is important to meditate to give your brain a rest. This will improve your health and your immune system."

I raised my hand and joked, "Will it also bring me wealth?"

My teacher answered, "Wisdom."

Mr. Byron finished the lesson with the fifth point.

He said, "(5) You can literally change your brain. Stop the negative and think positive."

Mr. Byron's lesson was done. It seemed as though it lasted all day. Yet, the day was still early as I walked to my next class.

Chapter 3

Biology

Biology was my next class, taught by my teacher, Mr. Best. His real name was not Mr. Best. We had given him that nickname because he was the best of all the teachers.

Before class started, I noticed some of my classmates writing notes on their hands to use for cheating on a test. Mr. Best began the biology lesson with a lecture about amoebas. We learned that amoebas are tiny bugs which are too small to view with the human eye alone. They live everywhere including inside the wood that our desks are made from.

Mr. Best backed up his facts by telling us about an experiment that had been done. He went on to tell us that amoebas live close to their families since this is where their food source is. If an amoeba wanders off, it will eventually return.

Mr. Best then pointed to me to ask if I understood the lesson.

"What did you learn?," asked the teacher.

"I learned that food is the most important resource," I said.

Mr. Best gave me a thumbs up. He then surprised the class with a pop quiz. My classmates always referred to me as the class wiz; therefore, I was not concerned about failing the test. I finished it quickly and returned it to my teacher just before the bell rang. My next class would soon begin. I was confident that I had passed.

Chapter 4

Health

My next class was Health. I found it to be the easiest class of all. That particular day, we were to learn about the negative facts of cigarette smoking.

The teacher, Mrs. Cooper, said "Smoking is broken down into two parts. It is (1) a habit and (2) an addiction. This is the reason why quitting is difficult."

She went on to say that it takes twenty-one days to break the habit because, by then, the chemicals have left the system.

"The addiction part is harder to cure. It can take months or years. These are reasons you all should fear ever picking up a cigarette," she said.

Mrs. Cooper let the class leave early so that she had time to go outside to smoke. She previously told us that she had tried a hundred times to quit and said that it is expensive. Her struggles taught us all to never buy cigarettes. It was then lunchtime. I reread my essay and had a hunch that I would get an "A".

Chapter 5

Math

Following lunchtime was Math class. The teacher allowed us to call him by his first name - Dave. He made learning the basics of finance fun by using money games. We were taught about the value of saving.

Dave began with the simple fact of subtracting expenses from income. He suggested that it was good behavior to save any leftover money.

"Once there is a good amount of savings, invest it in other accounts," said Dave.

He was always extremely serious. Even if someone made a joke, he would keep a straight face. Dave stated that money was the most important resource. I interrupted him and stated that food is the most important resource. He gave me a stern look and warned me that I would be written up if I had one more outburst. I wasn't the least bit concerned. My mind was consumed with the thought that money and food were both valuable resources, but that love was far above the most important.

The class ended. As I walked towards the door, I attempted to break through Dave's unplayful demeanor. I joked and asked him if we could be friends for a hundred grand.

Dave's eyebrows raised as he smiled and said, "Enjoy the rest of your day."

CHAPTER 6

History

The day's history lesson was about John F. Kennedy whose nickname was Jack. He became President of the United States in 1961. Tragically, he had been attacked by a bullet to the head. The history teacher, Miss Smart, went on to teach us that President Kennedy won the Purple Heart by saving sailors' lives while in the Navy. He also won the Pulitzer Prize for writing, "Profiles in Courage". He is the only president ever to have won this.

President Kennedy encouraged Americans to "Ask not what your country can do for you. Ask what you can do for your country". In a different speech, Kennedy said, "We choose to go to the moon". Miss Smart said that his life ended too soon. He had been shot in Dallas in 1963. She said there would be more to learn the following day, but for now the class was done. It was time to read my essay.

Chapter 7

English

I got myself situated at my desk when my English teacher called upon me to read my essay. The instructions were to write a long essay about war. I, however, crossed the line and wrote a short essay about love.

After walking to the front of the classroom, I began my speech.

I said, "The title of my essay is 'My Soul I Seek':

War is everywhere. It seems so surreal. We need to share love that is so real. Love grows stronger each time you give."

I had learned from Miss Woods that to get a point across, it is sometimes better to keep things short and simple. I received an "A" for my essay. My teacher said I was simply incredible and called me a class act!

Chapter 8

Home Room

The last day of school had finally arrived which happened to be a half day. The final exams were done. Soon it would be time for summer fun before my first semester of college. I would be attending a university out of state.

I was thrilled to have received the honor of being Valedictorian for having the highest grades of my classmates. As I walked into my Home Room, the students and teacher began applauding. They appeared to be proud of my accomplishments. My teacher, Miss Woods, then informed me that it was my responsibility to give a graduation speech. I hadn't previously thought about it, but she was right. It was my role being that I was head of my class.

As class was ending, Miss Woods waved goodbye and read her daily quote.

She said, "Never quit."

I was going to miss my teacher and her quotes. I wondered if I would always remember them. Though my mind was more concerned about the speech I was to write. There was only one week until graduation. I wanted to teach something profound within my speech. For now though, it was time for Finance class.

Chapter 9

Finance

Finance class was also taught by Dave. Since I found finance to be a cinch, I decided to major in it at college. Only a few students showed up to class on the last day. I thought that I, being Valedictorian, must be a role model and attend all of my classes.

Dave began his lesson by explaining compound interest. He called it the bread and butter of your earnings. He went on to say that interest is earned from savings accounts.

"The interest then begins to earn interest as well. The term for that is 'compounded interest'. That is how money works for you without doing anything. Here is an example:

You have 100 dollars and invest it into a savings account. Let's say that it earns 10 dollars of interest which adds up to 110. The 10 dollars is now earning interest as well. Let's say the 10 dollars of interest earns 1 dollar and the 100 earns 10 again. Your savings is then 121. You did nothing to earn 21 dollars. Now the 21 is also earning interest and so on and so on," said Dave.

He was good at explaining; however, Dave spoke in a monotone voice which made the lessons tiring. Next, I walked to Spanish class while eating a breakfast danish along the way. I had no time earlier to eat at home.

Chapter 10

Spanish

Being the last day of class, the Spanish teacher, Mrs. Garcia had arranged for my class to teach younger students Spanish. Earlier in the year, my teacher assigned a Spanish name to each student. Sophia was my Spanish name. Likewise, it was also my name in English.

Mrs. Garcia called upon me to lead the way in teaching.

I began by stating my name, saying, "Mi llamo Sophia. The two 'l's' together make a 'y' sound. Mi llamo Sophia means my name is Sophia."

Just then, a fourteen-year old student whom I was teaching told Mrs. Garcia that she understood.

I said, "E tu? Que llamo usted? Which means, 'What is your name?'"

I felt a bit rusty but I continued on with my lesson.

"Como este usted? Means how are you?"

Teaching Spanish to younger teenagers was rather fun to do. The class was done and the younger students said that Spanish was cool. We all said "goodbye" to Mrs. Garcia. She looked directly at me and gave me some words of advice.

Mrs. Garcia said, "Don't let life bring you down. Goodbye Sophia."

I left school and walked home with my friends. They wanted me to spend time with them, but I had a speech to write. They understood how important the speech was, so we agreed to get together over the summer.

High school was forever done. I sat alone writing my speech at home. I fought back the tears as it was hard to say goodbye.

Chapter 11

Graduation Speech

The day was Saturday which was the day I was to graduate. Before leaving home, I practiced my speech. I was to read it on stage underneath a dome. My speech was as such:

"Some would say that time spent in school is not the real world or a real life. A real life to them is being a father, mother, husband or wife. If that was true, then the graduating class this year would not be real and exist. School is real life and part of the real world. It is the place where we made friends that shared both good and bad times. Although it is sad to close this chapter, it is not the end. We are simply turning the page. High school taught us conditioning - to be like prisoners within the walls. Some would say we are now free; though, this is not true. As we begin new chapters, we have more decisions - a bigger world and a wider scope. When times get tough, we must set our visions small to cope, yet high to hope. The world is vast. Make choices that are wise like an owl. We are in charge of our own destinies. Let's do it in style. Goodbye classmates. I love you all. After you leave home, never forget to call your mother."

Thus, that was the speech I spent time writing. I was nearly in tears as I awaited the real world and for my real life to begin.

Chapter 12

Graduation Day

After stepping into my car wearing my graduation gown, I turned the music on loud. I only had to drive a short distance to the graduation ceremony. As I approached a red traffic light, I stopped the car and paused to rehearse my speech inside my head. The light turned green, but the traffic was at a dead halt. I remained cool, calm and collected.

Up ahead, I saw a person struggling in a pond. She and her car were submerged in water. I quickly called for an ambulance and ran towards the pond. People were standing at the edge of the pond staring, yet no one was offering any help. Some people were even leaving the scene. The events are somewhat of a blur; however, I do recall that my adrenaline kicked in and I jumped into the pond to save the woman.

As I grabbed onto the woman, I realized she was Miss Woods, my Home Room teacher. I pulled her out of the pond and placed her onto the ground. It was clear that she was nearly dead.

Miss Woods muttered, "I am dying."

Suddenly, I remembered her quotes.

I said "Miss Woods, never quit. You need to be trying."

Shortly after, the ambulance arrived. I had done all I could. The ambulance rushed Miss Woods away. I had spent so much time rescuing Miss Woods that I was late to graduation. I was only given a minute for my speech. I had just enough time to say, "Make each day count."

The high school principal stepped me aside. I was still in shock by the morning's events and not well intact. The principal only had one thing to say to me. He told me that I was, indeed, a class act!

Chapter 13

Beginning of College

Prior to attending college, I had spent the summer earning college credits in summer school. I passed with flying colors. The class was Music 101. I was never one to spend my time on trivial relationships. However, I met a boy named Troy during summer school and focused much of my attention on him.

Troy was one year younger than me, so he had one more year of high school. He enrolled in summer school to improve his grades. Troy had trouble with most of his classes, although he excelled in music. He thought that by taking music class, he could get an easy "A". He figured by doing so his parents would back off a bit and stop hounding him about his grades.

Troy was the lead singer in a rock band called the Treble with Men. I soon became aware of their music and quickly became their biggest fan. Troy and I became good friends right from the start.

By the time I entered college, I had lost interest in finance. I met with a guidance counselor who informed me that my grades were not at the level needed to continue my education at the university. I told the counselor I wanted to change my major from finance to music. The response was that I would be wasting my wealth of knowledge by doing so.

My grades continued to worsen. At the end of the semester, I had been ousted from the university. I left there and transferred to a local college to study music.

CHAPTER 14

Coming Home

I rode two trains on my way back home. I had two motives which were to spend time with Troy and to hopefully join his band someday. While being so far away from Troy, I feared losing him. We had turned our friendship into a relationship before I had left for college.

After moving back home, Troy and I had more time together. My parents were supportive of my decisions. They charged me to live with them, however.

Classes at the local college were set to begin on Monday. On the Sunday prior, I visited Miss Woods. She had survived her ordeal and was grateful to me for saving her life. By this time, she was no longer Miss Woods. She had gotten married; however, she still allowed me to call her Miss Woods.

I informed her that I had transferred to the local music college to follow my heart and make each day count. To my surprise, she had prepared an award for my heroism of saving her life.

Miss Woods and her husband asked if I would accept money for their gratitude. It was an awkward moment, but I said, "Yes". I knew I could surely use the help. I was astounded when I discovered the amount of money they gave me. It was enough to live off of for the rest of my life! I was in such shock that my body was trembling. I thanked and hugged both of them.

I had calmed down before stepping into my car to leave. I had to do a lot of deep breathing. After returning home, I went to bed so that I would be well rested for my first day at the local college.

CHAPTER 15

Piano

On Monday morning, I began my new college with Piano class. I was excited to learn even though my stomach was full of butterflies. Sitting in the front row, the teacher stood nearby as he began his lesson.

"There are seven notes for piano - C-D-E-F-G-A-B," he said.

The teacher went on to say, "The piano has 88 keys. The white keys are referred to as naturals and the black keys are called accidentals. The four most basic chords are major, minor, diminished and augmented. Once you pass this class, you will be able to write your own songs. There are twelve major and twelve minor triads. A triad refers to a three-note chord."

The piano teacher then asked if we were bored because some of the students were asleep. I raised my hand to tell my teacher that learning piano was grand. Unfortunately, I chose the wrong word because it caused him to go off in a tangent. He preached about how his grand piano was made by one of the world's best companies. I liked my teacher, but he sometimes seemed to drift away. We called him a nut which made him laugh.

When class was over, I had to run in order to get to my next class on time. My second class was Music Terminology.

Chapter 16

Music Terminology

Onto Music Terminology which I had been told was the key to learning music. I'm not sure if I was sold on that idea or not.

The teacher said, "We will learn one word from A-Z each day."

I thought that seemed simple.

He began with the letter "A" and said, "Allegro means lively or fast and allegretto is slightly slower. The next word is 'ballad'. It is a narrated story within a song. Next is the letter 'C'. We will learn 'cadenza' which is a song's solo section. For 'D' the word is 'drone' which is a note or chord played throughout a composition."

I was getting bored, although I was not alone. The other students were bored as well.

The teacher went on to say, "En pressant is the word for 'E'. It means hurrying forward."

I whispered to the classmate next to me and said, "I wonder if this class could hurry forward too."

The teacher overheard me and yelled directly at my face saying, "Not funny."

Fortunately, I had been blessed with a lot of self pride. Thus, I acted gracefully and remained silent.

The class was almost done. My joke created three new friends for me. After school, they asked me to hang out with them. I replied by saying that I would some other time since I had plans to spend time with Troy that day.

I only had two more classes until the day was done. I could then be with Troy. He had been waiting for me all day because he previously told me he had something to ask me. After my two classes were finished, Troy asked me to quit school and join the Treble with Men as the new lead singer.

Chapter 17

The Husband

It was a difficult decision to make. I would once again be leaving college; however, the band was already a huge success. I decided to join the Treble with Men. I seemed to blend in well.

One evening during rehearsal, Troy handed me a ring and said, "Marry me". Two years later, I became Troy's wife. Money was never an issue, as I was already set for life. We were able to live carefree.

Troy said he had a surprise for me. I knew it was a song. I told him I had a surprise for him as well.

I said, "It's where we both should be."

Troy said he had no clue. I called the band members to let them know we would be late to rehearsal. I motioned Troy to get into my car and we drove a short distance down the road.

I brought him to a brand new music studio and said, "It's yours."

Troy was ecstatic. He said he loved the studio and then said he had a song to sing to me. Before singing his song, he let me know that as his wife, I was the best part of his life. Troy then picked up the microphone and began singing. We were all alone but right where we belonged. The song was poetic and left a big impact on me. He then sang these words to me:

"You are a real class act!"

THE END